THE MURTOS
AR~~E MYSTERIOUS~~ . . .

As Ann and Alan were led away by the ape-like men called Murtos, Ann kept her courage alive with one thought: Jongor would save them . . .

Luckily, for Ann, she did not know that at that very moment, Jongor was hunting happily in the forest, without a thought of her or the Murtos.

Not only did Jongor not think of Ann—he could not even remember her. The terrible blow on the back of his head by a Murto's club had made him a victim of amnesia . . .

JONGOR FIGHTS BACK

by Robert Moore Williams

POPULAR LIBRARY • NEW YORK

Chapter I

The Murtos

"Watch out!" Jongor said.

At his words of warning, Ann and Alan Hunter stopped instantly. Their eyes ranged the jungle around them. Ahead was an open glade. Around them to the right and to the left were tall trees. In the far distance the tops of high mountains could be seen.

"I don't see anything," Ann Hunter said. Her voice betrayed her fear and rising anxiety.

"I don't see anything either," her brother answered. "But if Jongor says to watch out, you can bet he has a good reason for it."

The youth nodded toward the jungle man moving slowly and cautiously ahead. Jongor's broad, heavily muscled back was visible. He was moving forward very slowly, a spear ready in his right hand. He studied the ground in front of him, and now and then he would stand completely still in order to listen more intently. His manner indicated that he suspected the existence of danger very near but that he was as yet uncertain of what it was and where it was hiding.

In Lost Land, the first law of life was that danger was everywhere. Jongor had been born in Lost Land, the child of a naval aviator and his bride who had crashed in trying to fly across this enormous mountain wilderness in northern Australia. Having grown up here, Jongor knew the laws of life in this primitive region.

Across his back, he had slung the great bow that he always carried. The feathered ends of the arrows could be seen projecting from the quiver made of the skin of a wildcat. Around his middle was the single garment that he wore, a leopard breechcloth. On his left wrist, he wore a heavy bracelet made of solid gold which was set with a single large crystal.

Jongor did not know the secret of this bracelet and of the stone set in it—no one on Earth knew the real secret any more—but he had found the bracelet in Lost Land and he had learned how to use it.

Turning, he glanced at Ann and Alan Hunter. "You two stay there," he called out in a soft voice.

"Is something wrong?" Ann asked.

"I don't know—yet!" the jungle man replied. He waved one finger in the air, a motion for silence; then he began cautiously moving forward again.

Ann Hunter was visibly upset when she turned to speak.

"If we have more trouble getting out of Lost Land, I don't think I'll be able to stand it!"

Although her words indicated distress, her whole appearance was the exact opposite. She was clad in a miniskirt of deerskin, with matching moccasin-boots that reached her hips; the jungle man had made these for her when her own stout boots and whipcord riding breeches had been torn to shreds by rocks in the mountains and briars in the jungles. Her cheeks had that glow of perfect health, and she looked as if she was equal to any situation. The light rifle which she carried in two very capable brown hands made her look like a modern Diana of the woods come back to life.

"We're safer here in this wilderness than we would be back in the States," Alan commented. "Overloaded freeways, air pollution, jet liners crashing! The people back home are the ones who are living dangerously."

"I know," the young woman answered. "But I still want to go back, for a while at least. I know Jongor wants to see the land of his parents. Perhaps he will not want to live there all the time, but I think he should at least see his homeland—"

"The United States is not his homeland," Alan pointed out. "His homeland, the only world he has ever known, is right here in Lost Land. However, I do have to admit that this place is also trouble's natural home. Anybody who manages to enter Lost Land finds trouble here. If he tries to get out, he finds more trouble." The youth's voice was gloomy with foreboding. His eyes took in the vast semicircle of swamp and jungle. In front of them, in the far distance, tall, cloud-capped mountains marked the natural boundary of this lost country. Behind them, many miles away now, was the spot where the Murtos still lived in squalor in a vast ruined city that had once been, many thousands of years ago, a great mining town of the ancient Murians. Far to the right, at the edge of the mountains, Alan could dimly see the spot where the Arklans, the centaur people of lost antiquity, a race with the body of a small horse and the head, chest, and arms of a human, had once lived. And there they had also died, a race that had persisted in trying to follow outmoded traditional ways of life in spite of the fact that the rest of the world was going forward.*

"But maybe you will get to take your jungle man back to the United States and show him off to the girls at cocktail parties," Alan continued. "The girls will be very jealous when they see what a man you have caught."

"I haven't caught him!" Ann said, her voice tart.

"But you're working on it!" Alan continued.

"Oh, shut up!" Ann snapped at him.

Alan laughed. He knew his sister and Jongor were head over heels in love with each other. He also knew that the jungle man had no experience with women and had not even the faintest idea of the meaning of being in love. "You can teach him about love," Alan continued. "That'll be a switch! Usually it's the man who teaches the ignorant, uneducated female—"

"I said for you to shut up!" Ann repeated.

Alan laughed again and knowing how far he could go

* See THE RETURN OF JONGOR, by Robert Moore Williams, published by Popular Library.

in teasing his sister, changed the subject. "Anyhow, I'm
very glad Jongor is with us. When he's along we've really
got nothing to worry about. He'll get us out of Lost
Land!"

His frank appraisal of the tall, muscular man armed
with the spear and bow and arrows, was based on past
experience. He and Ann had both seen this jungle man in
action. They had seen such miracles as the swamp dinosaurs, still surviving here in this wilderness, not only
obey him but also come to him to have their noses
rubbed! They had seen him fight the whole tribe of Murtos. They had seen him enter the city of the Arklans and
emerge alive when this strange race of centaur people
had blown themselves off the Earth.

Ann was silent, musing on the incredible adventures
that had taken place here. Alan had come here, on an exploring trip. When he had not returned, she had come
here trying to find and rescue him. The Blackfellows
who lived in the deserts around Lost Land had attacked
her expedition. A strange voice had spoken from the air
telling the aborigines to attack. Eventually she had been
rescued by a strange man from the jungle—Jongor! * But
before this rescue, she had been captured by the Murtos
and had been held prisoner in their vast, ruined city.
Then she and Jongor and Alan had been on their way
out of Lost Land when a strange message had come
from an even stranger creature who had called herself
Nesca, Queen of the Arklans, asking for help. Since she
had once saved Jongor's life, a call from her for help was
a sacred obligation to the man from the jungle. Jongor
never deserted his friends. Eventually they discovered
that the message had been a fake but not before they
found themselves watching the end of these centaur people—and almost their own end, too!

"This happened to me!" Ann said, as she remembered
what had taken place here in this strange world. Lost
Land was like an enormous island where the primitive
conditions of hundreds of thousands of years ago still existed. Here also were to be found creatures that in some

* See JONGOR OF LOST LAND by Robert Moore Williams,
published by Popular Library.

instances had become extinct in the rest of the world for millions of years: dinosaurs, for one, pterodactyls, for another. The pterodactyls were Nature's first experiment with birds. They did not possess true feathers and they could not rise from the ground and fly, but they could launch themselves from heights and could glide through the air on enormous flapping wings for long distances.

Probably there were other strange creatures in this incredible world that she had not seen, she thought.

Looking ahead, she could see Jongor. Into her mind came the thought that in many ways the jungle man was stranger than anything else that was here. She recalled the history of his life as he had told it to her. When he was twelve years old, the pterodactyls had killed his parents. How great a punishment Jongor had inflicted on them because of that! Left an orphan in a dawn world, Jongor had learned the law of survival the hard way. When running had been necessary, he had learned to run. When cunning had been indicated, he had learned cunning. Because strength was always needed, strength of muscle, of mind, and of emotion, he had gained strength, doing all of this without realizing he was doing it. Where danger lurked at every waterhole and death hid behind almost every bush, the boy had grown into manhood and had become a brown-skinned, stalwart giant. He had made friends with the dinosaurs, controlling them through the crystal in the bracelet he wore on his left wrist, and these gigantic swamp monsters had been his companions and playmates.

Tens of thousands of years in the past, Lost Land was a colony of a vast civilization that had once existed on the islands of the Pacific. Indeed, a continent had existed there. The continent and the islands had been the homelands of the Murians.

When the continent and many of the islands went down thousands of years in the past, the colony of Murian miners in Lost Land were permanently cut off from its homeland.

Jongor knew the degenerate descendents of this past civilization as the Murtos. He regarded them as animals and they called him *the wild beast from the jungle.*

Ann knew that these monkey-men still possessed some of the scientific achievements of the great race from which they had sprung. The crystal in the bracelet which Jongor used to control the dinosaurs was one of those great achievements. It had been made by a Murian scientist long ago and had been lost in this wilderness. Had the ancient Murians used the dinosaurs as work horses to clear the jungle? Ann did not know the answer to this question. She did know, however, that although the Murtos still possessed some of the science of their forefathers, it was now a degenerate science, used by rote, with no real understanding of the principles involved. A broken tool, or a broken weapon, was to them a tool or a weapon to be thrown away. They no longer had the knowledge needed for the repairs. The Murtos had sunk so low that eventually the only weapons they had left were clubs, spears, and knives. They no longer had the know-how to make even bows and arrows.

"All of this happened to just me!" Ann Hunter thought, as she watched Jongor. "I got to come to Lost Land! I got to find Jongor!"

Secretly, she was very thrilled by all that had happened to her.

One of the smaller details of Jongor's history that pleased her was how he got his name. His parents had named him John. They had tried to teach him to say his full name—John Gordon. His childish efforts to say his own name had inevitably resulted in Jongor. So Jongor he had become, to his adoring parents. Now in his early twenties, he continued to think of himself, simply, as Jongor.

Watching him, Ann Hunter knew that in this giant much of the small boy still remained. Somehow, she hoped it would always remain in him, the small boy who took delight in simple things, in sharp sticks and shining stones—and in castles in the sky.

"I don't see or hear anything," Ann said to her brother. She shifted the light rifle she carried in the crook of her arm. "But just in case there is something here that I don't hear or see—"

"You can bet there is something," her brother said. "When you don't see or hear anything bad in this country, that's the time to be extra careful. Hey, Sis, look! Just ahead of Jongor there!" His voice had risen sharply, and he was pointing above Jongor's head.

Jongor had stopped moving. Spear ready in his hand, he was poised as motionless as a shadow. Ahead of him was jungle growth perhaps ten feet tall.

The tops of the growth were shaking.

"Something's coming through the trees!" Ann whispered.

"What is it, an elephant?" Alan asked.

"I've never heard Jongor mention an elephant here in Lost Land," Ann said.

"To make that much of a commotion it must be almost as big as an elephant," Alan said. "You don't just walk through brush that thick and that tall! What I mean is, to force your way through that growth, you've got to be strong!"

The brush parted. Out of it came what looked like a man, except that it was about nine feet tall!

Adding to the impression of height was an ostrich-plumed metal helmet on his head, a helmet that was shaped a little like those worn by the Greek legions that had marched under Alexander. In fitting with the helmet, the giant was wearing a suit of chain mail armor that dropped in a kind of loose tunic to his hips and extended downward to his feet in the form of a suit of tights. His arms and hands were covered with the same kind of close-linked chain mail armor.

In his hands he held a heavy two-bladed battle axe. He had no other weapon.

If he could get close enough to use his axe, he would need no other weapon.

Emerging from the brush, he stopped and stood staring at Jongor.

In his turn, Jongor stared at the giant.

"Where—where'd that monster come from?" Alan Hunter gasped.

"How would I know?" his sister answered. "Anything

that ever existed on Earth may still exist here in Lost
Land!"

"But giants never existed—"

"There are stories of them in the Bible!"

"Legends—"

"Most legends are always somewhere based on fact!"
Ann Hunter answered. *"Jongor! Get away from that
monster!"*

Standing his ground, the jungle man did not answer.
He was mystified and curious. A Murto had once told
him about giants that lived up near the timberline but he
had paid little attention. Here was proof that there was
some kind of truth in what he had regarded as a fanciful
story. However, he was not afraid of this giant. Instead,
if he got the opportunity, he thought he would like to
talk to the big creature, if he could speak its language, or
learn its tongue—that is, if he could not already speak it.
He was ready to fight, if he had to, but he preferred not
to fight.

Dropping the point of his spear to the ground, he
lifted his right hand with the empty palm extended forward in the ancient gesture of friendship.

Lifting the battle axe over his head, the giant moved
ponderously toward him.

The huge creature wanted war, not peace.

Gripping his spear in both hands, Jongor stood his
ground.

"Peace, Great One," he said, in the tongue of the
Murtos.

Grunting a negative answer, the giant kept coming.

"Jongor!" Ann Hunter screamed. She lifted her rifle.
The giant was wearing armor and probably thought
himself safe. This indicated he had no knowledge of the
penetrating power of a slug from a modern high-
powered sporting rifle, a slug that moved just under
3,000 feet per second. The giant would soon discover his
error.

As for Jongor, if he had no more sense than to stand
and fight a giant in an armor that would probably turn
the point of his spear, she would do what she could to

protect him. Stepping to one side to get the jungle man out of the line of fire, she centered the sights on the right leg of the advancing giant. She did not wish to kill him. All she wanted to do was stop him.

Perhaps just the sound of the gun would do that! With this thought in her mind, she changed her target again, aiming the rifle at the heavy plumes atop the helmet of the giant.

Her eyes went along the sights but she did not fire the gun.

A thrown club that seemed to come from nowhere struck the rifle just ahead of the trigger guard. The club was heavy enough to knock the gun from her fingers. However, the weapon deflected the course of the club and it slammed into her face, sending her stumbling backward.

If it had struck with the full force of its blow, it could easily have killed her. But the rifle had absorbed part of its force. Probably this fact saved her life.

As she stumbled backward, she turned startled eyes in the direction from which the club had come. What she saw there shook her worse than the blow from the club!

"Murtos!" she screamed.

Out of the trees on the right, the degenerate monkeymen were dropping to the ground. Some had clubs, some had spears. All were charging directly toward her.

She knew instantly that the appearance of the giant had been planned. The Murtos and the giant were working together. While the giant attracted Jongor's attention —and possibly killed him—the Murtos intended to capture her. This was a trap!

Beside her, she heard Alan swear one mighty "Damn!" then lift up his rifle and fire. One quick shot and a charging Murto went down.

Alan had had time to fire one shot, no more, before the wave of charging Murtos were upon them.

"Jongor!" Ann screamed.

She saw him turn his head in her direction, one quick glance. As if this moment of inattention was exactly what he was waiting for, at the instant Jongor turned his head in response to her scream, the armor-clad giant rushed forward and struck downward with his heavy axe straight at Jongor's head.

One glimpse she got—and no more. She did not see the axe strike Jongor. All she knew was that she was knocked down and that a Murto fell on top of her.

Chapter II

Captives!

Advancing through the open glade, Jongor had expected to find a group of Murtos hiding in the heavy growth. His keen ears had caught a slight sound which indicated the presence of the monkey-men of Lost Land. He had no fear of them. His purpose was to flush them out of hiding and send them running. Murtos in hiding could become a menace. Murtos in the open were Murtos in flight!

When the giant came striding out of the thicket, Jongor was thoroughly surprised. So the Murto who had talked to him of such creatures had been telling the truth!

"Peace, Great One," Jongor said.

A split second later, the sound of a rifle shot came from behind him. He glanced around. One glimpse told him that he and Ann and Alan had walked into a trap. He saw the Murtos come tumbling from the trees and rush toward Ann and Alan. Out of the corner of his eyes, he saw the giant rush toward him.

Jongor would have turned back to fight the Murtos but the giant was upon him. To take the time needed to turn and run would mean the axe would split his body from head to toe. All he could do was turn his body to one side. Within inches of his head, the axe whistled

15

past. It struck the spear that he was trying to get out of the way and cut through the stout shaft as if it had been a twig. As he realized he was missing his target, the grunting giant tried to turn the direction of the axe. He was too late for this. Missing Jongor's toes by perhaps an inch, the axe sunk deep into the ground.

"Uh!" the astounded giant grunted. His brain worked slowly and he did not understand how he could have missed. His intended victim was almost three feet shorter than he was. His victim was a pygmy! Since the Murtos had promised him a fine reward for eliminating this pygmy, he had intended to get the job done quickly and neatly, to collect the reward of promised diamonds, and to return to his home section of Lost Land. Now, somehow, he had missed and his axe was buried in the ground. He tried to jerk it free. It was stuck, probably in a root. However, the axe did not really matter. The blow had cut through the spear shaft of the pygmy and the creature was now unarmed.

Bong!

The pygmy struck him on the side of the helmet with the butt-end of the spear. The roaring sound almost deafened the giant. He stumbled backward, his hands going up to protect his head. The pygmy used the end of the spear to stick him in the stomach, hard.

The blunt end of the wooden shaft did not penetrate the linked mail but it hit the armor so hard that the giant thought his stomach was shoved clear through his spine. Worse still, it knocked most of the wind out of the giant. Grabbing his stomach with both hands, he doubled up. Promptly the spear landed again on the helmet. The bonging roar of the hard wood on metal almost drove the giant out of his mind.

"Jongor!" Ann Hunter's voice came from behind.

This was a sound that would always turn the jungle man. He turned now, as the giant snatched for his buried axe and tried to jerk it free.

Turning, Jongor saw that Ann and Alan Hunter were on the ground under what looked like a swarm of Murtos. Whether they were dead or not, he could not tell.

Ann had had enough life left to call to him. How long she would have that much life he did not know. He started toward her, to help.

One of the Murtos saw him coming. Great Orbo, their leader. Leaping to his feet, Orbo pointed at Jongor. "Get the jungle beast!"

Leaving Ann and Alan to be subdued by two Murtos, the others leaped to obey the orders of their leader.

Already the great bow was off Jongor's back. He strung it with a single quick motion. So swift was his hand that the arrow seemed to leap from the quiver to the bowstring.

"Come and get me, you howling monkeys!" he shouted at them.

A spear was thrown. Jongor dodged it. In reply, he released an arrow. The throat of the Murto who had thrown the spear sprouted feathers. The others hesitated.

"Get him!" Orbo yelled. "Two extra wives for the one who catches him!"

The Murtos moved forward again. Orbo signalled to the trees on his right. His reserve force, held there for such an emergency, began dropping to the ground. Pointing at Jongor, Orbo screamed orders at them.

Jongor nocked another arrow on the string. "Come and get me, you with tails!" he shouted at them. One Murto, a dozen Murtos, he could handle. However, as the reserve force began to drop from the trees, he realized that it was not a dozen Murtos he was facing, but fifty!

They came at him now in a howling flood. Near him, the incredible giant had finally succeeded in freeing his battle axe from the ground.

At this moment, no matter how much he would have preferred to do otherwise, the jungle man knew he had to face one of the facts of life he had learned in Lost Land, namely, when you can't win, run and fight another day!

If he could get away—and this was by no means sure— he could find some way to rescue Ann and Alan from the Murtos.

The giant was swinging the axe again. Jongor sent an

arrow at the giant's middle. The shaft glanced harmlessly away from the linked chain mail. And Jongor turned to run.

A scream went up from the Murtos as he turned. How they had longed in the past to see this strange jungle beast—to them, a human was a strange beast—turn and run. The sight made them feel more important than they had ever felt in all of their lives!

"Spear him!" Orbo yelled. "Don't let him get away!"

Jongor knew better than to run without looking back. The spears he saw coming, he dodged. But as he glanced quickly ahead to make certain there were no obstacles directly in front of him, a thrown club hit him a heavy blow on the back of his head just at the base of the brain.

He went down. Blackness closed in over him.

For only an instant, the blackness lasted. Then it was gone and he was on his feet again and running for his life as he had learned to do when he was a boy growing up in the wilderness of Lost Land. Again his feet had wings. Again it seemed to him that he could fly as fast as he had when he was a boy. Flying along the ground, he laughed as he ran, strange laughter that jeered at the slower Murtos and told them they could not run fast enough to catch him.

If any damage had been done to his brain by the thrown club, the damage did not slow his legs.

He outran the slower Murtos. When they gave up the chase, he kept running. Even after they had returned to their two captives, Jongor continued to run. As he ran, he laughed. His laugh was the shrill high laughter of a child.

Ann Hunter stumbled as she walked. She had a reason for stumbling. This reason lay in the fact that her hands were tied behind her back with a slippery skin rope that was held tightly by the Murto following her. Walking beside her, Alan Hunter stumbled, for the same reason.

Ann could not get her hands to her face, to wipe away the tears from her eyes. Consequently, she let them run down her cheeks.

The tears were the result of utter frustration. Now that the Murtos had captured her again, she felt that she would never escape from Lost Land.

Even worse than capture by the monkey-men was the utterly shameful fact that Jongor had run away and had left her to be captured. Deep in the heart of Ann Hunter, deep in the heart of every woman, was the wishful thought that her man would never run from danger. She knew, of course, that the odds against Jongor had been so heavy that the only way he could have helped her was to run. To face all of the Murtos, with that axe-swinging giant ready to take a hand in the fight, had been to invite sudden death. This, she understood. It was only that somewhere deep inside her mind, in the place where the wishful fantasies dwell, she had hoped that her man was big enough to stand against the whole world. That this was pure fantasy, and utter nonsense, she also knew. She knew the real reason Jongor had run away had been to give himself the chance to return later and rescue her.

"You didn't expect him to stand there and get his skull split wide open, did you?" Alan asked, beside her. "Even Jongor can't lick all the Murtos in Lost Land, in addition to that—to that—" Pausing, he groped for words to describe the giant striding along ahead of them. "—to that monster!"

Calazao, the giant was walking at the head of the column with Great Orbo. Calazao was carrying the battle axe on his shoulder. He was talking freely, in a voice that was half grumble and half mutter, in the language of the Murtos to Great Orbo. Ann and Alan both understood a little of the Murto talk.

"How did he ever dodge my axe?" the giant was complaining. "It must have been that a forest devil turned the edge aside at the last moment!" Calazao was greatly pleased with this deduction. It released him from the charge of missing his target. "Yes! A devil helped him. That is the explanation. The next time I catch him, he will not escape me!"

"The next time you see him, you will probably run so fast your shadow won't be able to keep up with you!" Ann Hunter shouted. This kind of talk angered her.

"Shhh, Sis!" Alan protested. "A minute ago you were crying because Jongor had run away and now you're telling that giant what Jongor will do when he returns!"

Calazao and Great Orbo turned to look at the young woman.

"So he is coming back, is he?" the giant boomed the question at her. "So I will run from him, will I? Ho!" Calazao swung the axe around his head again, alarming Great Orbo and Alan Hunter.

"Sometimes it pays to keep your mouth shut, Sis!" Alan said. "Calazao will be on the watch for Jongor now, as will all the Murtos."

"They would be on the watch anyhow," Ann answered. "Jongor is the one they really want, not me. The only reason they want me is to use me as bait for a trap for Jongor!" As she spoke, she stopped moving.

"Get along, you!" the Murto holding the rope told her. He emphasized his command by jerking on the skin rope. This pulled her off her feet. She fell heavily.

"Get up, you!" the Murto said, kicking her. The fact that he was not wearing shoes made no difference. Any Murto could kick heavily and expertly with the ball of his foot.

"Oh!" Ann gasped, in pain.

The sight sent Alan Hunter into a violent rage. "You jerk her off her feet, then you kick her for falling! If I only had my rifle!"

Weaponless, his hands tied behind his back, Alan Hunter used the only weapon he had—his head. He butted the Murto in the stomach.

The monkey-man fell over backward. Momentarily, he dropped his club, but when he had scrambled to his feet, he had recovered it again. Suddenly violent rage gleamed in his close-set animal eyes.

"I'll fix you for this!" he shouted.

The commotion attracted the attention of Great Orbo who left off talking to Calazao and hurried to the scene.

"Stop it, Kego!" Orbo shouted.

"He butted me with his head!" Kego answered.

"So what?"

"But he hit me!" the enraged Murto protested.

"I'm going to hit you if you don't shut up and get back on the job of holding the ropes!" Orbo told him. "And if I hit you, even your grandchildren will remember it!" Orbo lifted his club.

Thus confronted with his huge chief, Kego's rage subsided into muttered sounds about what he would do to these two humans at some later date.

"If you do anything to anybody without my orders, I'll have your tail cut off!" Orbo told him.

This silenced Kego completely. Among the Murtos, the length and the furry quality of the tail were of great importance in determining social position. Males with the longest, bushiest tails got the best women! A male with no tail at all was lucky if he even got enough to eat!

Glaring at Alan, Kego tenderly helped Ann to her feet. The march was resumed.

"Where are you taking us?" Ann asked Great Orbo.

The Murto leader ignored her question. He moved again to the head of the column.

"They're taking us back to their city," Alan said. In his voice gloom was inches deep.

In physical appearance, the Murtos were shorter than the average human but were much more heavily built. Their squat, muscular bodies were covered with thin, soft fur. They were not as heavy as gorillas but in other ways, they much resembled those huge apes. The size and the shape of their heads indicated an almost human intellectual capacity—almost but not quite. They looked like beasts that had started to become men but then had found the evolutionary trail too long and too hard and had sought the easier way of turning back to apes. Their resemblance to animals was further increased by their long bushy tails.

Among the Murtos not only was the possession of a longer, bushier tail a mark of achievement but it also entitled its owner to the respect of all other Murtos. Great Orbo, the leader of this group, had a tail that was long enough to curl around his neck. It was also extremely bushy. There was not a Murto alive who did not envy Orbo his wonderful tail.

"Move faster!" Kego said, behind Ann and Alan.

"I'm moving as fast as I can!" she answered. Actually, she had been moving as slowly as she could, watching the jungle on both sides, serenely confident that even if Jongor had run away, he would run back later and would rescue her at the right time. She had little doubt that this gray-eyed jungle man, who had managed to survive here in the vast treacherous hell of Lost Land, could accomplish anything he set his mind to doing.

Umber, the second in command of the group, came past her, moving from the rear to the head of the column. Umber, whose tail was only a little shorter and a little less furry than Orbo's, paused to stare at her.

"Female, how would you like to belong to me?" Umber questioned Ann.

"I'd rather be dead," the miserable young woman answered.

Umber grinned at her.

"You get on about your business!" Alan Hunter said to him.

Rage instantly formed a red film in the Murto's eyes. Nobody was going to talk to him like that, particularly not a skinless human beast! Lifting the spear he carried, he brought the flat of the blade down on Alan's skull.

The youth collapsed instantly. Umber lifted his spear again, the point downward this time.

"You leave him alone!" Ann screamed. Her hands tied behind her back, she did the only thing she could do, she threw herself face down over her brother's body, leaving Umber no choice except to strike her in the back if he wanted to strike Alan. "Orbo will have your tail if you hurt him!"

At her words, Umber glanced hastily toward the head of the column. Up there, Orbo had heard Ann's scream and was looking back. Standing beside Orbo, the giant had taken his axe from his shoulder.

"I meant no harm," Umber said, placatingly. Forgetting all about the mission that was taking him to the head of the column, he retreated hastily to the rear of the line of straggling monkey-men.

"Are you badly hurt, Alan?" Ann whispered to her brother.

"No, but I'm mad as hell!" Alan answered. "Get off of me so I can find out how badly I am hurt."

Alan got slowly to his feet. His fingers ran tenderly along his skull where the flat of the spear blade had landed, then he looked back along the line of Murtos to where Umber had disappeared. "Some day I'm going to catch that Umber and give him a knock on the noggin, too!" he muttered. "Stop worrying about me, Sis! I'm all right!"

"Move along, both of you!" Kego said, jerking on the skin ropes.

"Give him a chance to rest for a few minutes!" Ann said, her voice hot.

Kego gestured toward the front of the line. "When Orbo says to march, we march," he said.

"But Alan may be hurt!"

"He will be hurting worse if he does not obey Orbo," Kego answered. "Walk!"

"But—"

"Shut up, Sis, before you get me killed," Alan said. "I can walk." He began to move ahead.

Up ahead, Great Orbo and Calazao were engaged in spirited talk. The giant was having difficulty in understanding some of the more spiritual aspects of Murto philosophy and Orbo was explaining these to him.

"I have made up my mind about the woman," Orbo said. "She will be the bride of the sun. This was decided long ago, only she escaped, with the help of that jungle beast you told us you would destroy—"

"And so I will, the next time I meet him!" the giant answered.

"Or if the Great Lost God should speak and claim her, she would go to him!" Orbo said, repressing a shudder.

"Why do you shake like that?" the giant asked him.

"We always do that when we mention the Great Lost God," Orbo explained. "It is a mark of respect."

"It looks to me like the mark of fear," Calazao said. "Is this Great Lost God so terrible that even to think of him makes you Murtos shiver?"

"Yes, but don't say such things aloud," Orbo answered, looking quickly around. "He may be listening!"

Hearing this talk, Ann Hunter shuddered. These creatures were sun worshippers, their god was the flaming light that moved across the sky each day. To become the bride of the sun meant being burned alive on the altar of the sun, the sun's rays being brought to focus on the body of the sacrifice by a huge leans which could produce a temperature of thousands of degrees. She did not know what the Great Lost God was—and she did not want to learn.

"That is what she will be, unless I change my mind," Orbo continued. "I mean, unless the gods will otherwise," he hastily added. "Or unless she is not perfect enough for them."

"What then?" Calazao rumbled.

"Oh, then I shall keep her for myself," Orbo answered.

"It looks as if whichever way it goes, you are going to get the raw end of the deal, Sis," Alan Hunter said.

"I heard them," Ann answered. Again her eyes swept the jungle around her, looking for Jongor. "He'll come," she told herself over and over again. "He'll find us!"

Chapter III

Jongor in a Strange Land

It was well for Ann Hunger that she could not see the jungle man at this moment. In her mind was the sure thought that he was somewhere near her, watching and waiting for a chance to rescue her. If she could have seen what he was really doing she would not have believed it.

He was leisurely stalking a deer in an open glade. His manner was completely relaxed. He stopped to watch ants scurrying about their nest, seeming to find in the antics of the little insects much that was of interest to him. When his stomach reminded him that it was hungry, he remembered the deer, and resumed his stalk of it. Again he was distracted, this time by a small and quite harmless green snake in a bush. Reminded again by his stomach that he was hungry, he started for the deer, only to be distracted again, this time by a grumbling ant-eater that came wandering by. When the ant-eater had passed, he resumed his stalk of the deer.

In his mind was the vague thought that he was hungry, nothing more, and that the deer would make an appetizing meal. In his mind was no thought whatsoever of Ann or Alan Hunter. So far as he was concerned, they had never existed.

He had no memory of them!

The club thrown by the Murto that had struck him on the back of the head and had knocked him down had almost cracked his skull, with the result that pressure had been set up deep within the gray matter of the brain. His memory had slipped back into the past. He could remember his childhood and his parents perfectly. He could remember with complete clarity the events of his life in Lost Land, *up to the last year*.

It was during the past year that he had met Ann and Alan Hunter. He had no memory of ever knowing them. He was simply Jongor, the youth who had grown up in Lost Land, the youth who had lived by his wits, his cunning, the speed in his legs, and the strength in his muscles.

It is a strange characteristic of the human mind that as a result of a blow, the mind will sometimes regress into the past. For recent events there may be complete amnesia. A person injured in an accident may not be able to recall any of the events leading up to the accident. However he might remember the day before the accident, or the week before it, or the year before it.

Lost memories may be recovered. Or they may not. A person may live for many years with a great gap in his memory—and never know the gap is there. Another characteristic of this condition is that the gap is concealed. The individual himself does not know that a part of his memory is gone, is lost from sight, and cannot be recalled.

Jongor did not know that he had lost a part of his memory. Deep in his brain he was sometimes aware of a dull ache. Ever so often he shook his head at the ache, thinking that this might make it go away. Now and then he scratched his head for the same reason. Neither head shaking nor scratching relieved the ache. It did not go away, but on the other hand, it did not become any stronger either. He soon learned to ignore it. He was also aware of a vague fleeting picture that from time to time tried to emerge into his consciousness. This was the image of a young woman. His impression was that this was a memory image of his mother. He could remember his mother quite clearly and with great warmth and affection. She was the only woman he had ever known. He had many memory images of her, happy, laughing, and gay.

Or had he known another young woman? Had he really known someone else who looked like his mother but who was not his mother? How could this be true? How could another woman who resembled his mother ever have found her way into Lost Land? He shook his head at his own question, then tried to think, wrinkling his forehead in the process. Thinking was so difficult! His brain seemed filled with some kind of an oily substance, with the result that he could not get a firm grip on any thought he wanted. Like eels, the thoughts slipped out of his grasp.

The image of the young woman slipped out of sight in the same way. It left behind it a sort of haunted longing, a kind of dim sadness.

Finally, all that was left within his mind was the vague knowledge of hunger. At the sight of the deer in range of his great bow, he forgot everything except the fact that he was hungry.

Unaware of danger in its world, the deer was feeding quietly. In the recesses of leafy growth, Jongor carefully fitted an arrow to the string. The bow stave creaked as he drew the feathered end of the shaft to his right ear.

"Fly straight," he whispered to the arrow, as he released it. As if it had heard the words, the arrow seemed to obey him, leaping straight at the deer.

Struck just behind the shoulder, the animal gave a great bound, that single convulsive leap that often comes when the death blow has been taken. High the deer leaped, heavily it fell. It did not move after it had struck the ground.

The arrow had penetrated its heart.

Jongor cut succulent steaks from the carcass, sought a secluded spot. He found one where his back was protected by the overhang from a high cliff and where he could see in all directions, and gathered twigs. Here in this place he had built a small fire many times before but never before had he started a fire with a small cigarette lighter which he took from the pocket in his loincloth.

Without a moment's hesitation, he used the lighter. At the scrape of the flint, the little flame leaped up. When the twigs had caught, he slipped the lighter back into the pocket in his loincloth.

He did not wonder how the lighter worked or why it worked or even where he had gotten it. To him, its function was pure magic. It worked the same way the arrow worked, because he wanted it to work, because he told it to function.

He did not remember that Alan Hunter had given him the little lighter as a present less than a month before. In his world at this time, there was no Alan Hunter. And no Ann Hunter. There was, however, a little gadget that worked by pure magic which could be used to start a fire.

The multi-veined crystal which he wore in the bracelet on his left arm was another such magical device, except he knew where he had gotten it. He also knew that if he concentrated his attention on it, the great beasts of the swamp that he called *dinos* would hear his voice and would obey his orders.

Dinner finished, he squatted beside the fire. In the tiny blaze, which now had died to a bed of coals except for little flickers of flame, was companionship and friendship. When a fire was burning, he felt a little less lonely in this vast wilderness called Lost Land. Squatting with his back against the wall, he nodded there. The image of the woman came again into his mind. Somehow he had the impression that she needed him. Or was it the other way around, did he need her? He did not know which was which. Perhaps they needed each other!

Before he could find a clear answer to the puzzle, the image had slid out of his mind again. He called out to the image and tried to catch it in his hands, so real was it, but it eluded his clutching fingers. Coming to full wakefulness, he felt very foolish. Then he realized what had awakened him.

Sounds in the distance. Not animal sounds, not Murto noises. The click of metal on metal. Such a sound as could only be made by men!

Jongor did not pause to consider how he knew the

kind of sounds that men made. He was curious about them. Perhaps, somewhere inside, he was hungry for the companionship of his own kind.

Slipping the great bow on his back, he picked up the spear and moved in the direction of the sounds he had heard.

The two men had made a hasty camp at the edge of a bluff. Above them, rising in a series of tiers, was a cliff that joined itself solidly to the mountain above it. In front of them was a rocky glade where no vegetation grew and where no one could approach unseen. This much precaution they had taken.

What little camp equipment they had was scattered about. It was not much in the way of equipment. A medicine kit in a leather case, an ammunition box, and two smaller metal boxes which apparently contained food. Or which had contained it. In addition, each had a rainproof plastic bag slung over his shoulder.

Two high-powered sporting rifles rested against the wall of the ledge above them.

They had built a fire and were roasting chunks of venison over it. The deer from which the venison had been taken they had found dead, of an obvious arrow wound, and partly butchered. They had helped themselves to the carcass.

"Better than making our own kill," Gnomer, the taller of the two said.

"I only hope the native who shot that deer doesn't come back for more of his kill," Rouse said. As he ate, he watched the glade below them.

Gnomer reached out and patted his rifle. "Let him come back," Gnomer said. "He is probably a Blackfellow. Right now, after the way the Blackfellows deserted us, I would be willing to shoot on sight the next native I see." Anger sounded in Gnomer's voice as he spoke. He was a tall man, ruggedly built, with square broad shoulders and cold gray eyes.

In America in the old days, this man would have been a prospector, or a claim jumper, depending on which occupation offered the biggest gain at the moment. He would have been a cattle baron, if raising cattle had been the way to make it big, but if rustling had promised the biggest gain, he would have been a cattle thief. In the era when the railroads were built, he would have been a railroad magnate. If he had lived during the days of the big oil booms, he would have been a wild-cat driller. Or a wild-cat speculator.

Whatever his occupation, woe to the man who had tried to stand in the way of Jake Gnomer!

"Yeah!" Rouse answered. Shorter than Gnomer and not nearly as broad in the shoulders, he was a faithful reproduction of the bigger man but done on a smaller scale. "If I ever get one of those wild devils between my sights, there's going to be one less in this section!"

"You'll catch one, if talk will do it!" Gnomer answered. "If you had been on the watch, like I told you, they would never have had a chance to slip away from us."

"I couldn't help it because I fell asleep," Rouse grumbled in his throat. "I was watching 'em close. Maybe I nodded. I swear I didn't close my eyes but maybe I did close 'em for a minute or two, while you were scouting the pass into this place. Suddenly, no bearers. I still don't understand how they could have slipped away so quietly."

"You probably closed your eyes for a couple of hours!" Gnomer said, bitterness in his voice. "While you were nodding, they had time to take most of our gear and clear out. They also got our map case!"

In his voice, anger was suddenly hot. "Damn it, Rouse, I ought to put a bullet through you for letting them get away with our maps!"

Rouse concentrated his attention on his chunk of venison. He did not like the tone of Gnomer's voice. He liked even less the words Gnomer was using. He tried to shrug away his own failure as being unimportant.

"What difference does it make?" he questioned. "We got here all right, didn't we?" His gesture conveyed the idea that all of their problems had been solved.

"We got here," Gnomer conceded. "But now that we're here, we don't know where to go because you let the porters steal our maps!"

"Umh!" Rouse grunted, almost choking on a bite of venison. "But Jake, now that we're here, we're a cinch to find what we're looking for. It's got to be here somewhere. We'll find it easy, now that we're here."

Jake Gnomer swept his free hand in an arc that included the whole of Lost Land. "You see how big this place is? Without a map, we can hunt for years without finding what we are looking for."

"Well, I didn't lose the maps on purpose," Rouse answered. "Just give us a couple of weeks here and we'll find it. You just wait and see if I'm not right."

"You better be right," Gnomer said. "Or I'm likely to go back without you!"

Rouse was silent. Fear suddenly was dwelling heavily within his eyes.

As quietly as a moving shadow, Jongor came down the series of ledges above the two men. He could move through thick jungle growth with an effortless ease that left no trace of his passage, slipping through tangles like a great cat. Coming down the series of ledges was easy for him. He reached the ledge directly above the two men without either knowing that he existed.

At the sight of them, at the sound of their talk, something akin to hunger stirred in him. However, his belly was full and he could not be hungry for food. What, then, was this feeling that came into existence inside him at the sight of these two men?

Although he did not know it, the feeling in him was hunger, but not for food. Instead it was hunger for the companionship of his own kind.

While the memory of Ann and Alan Hunter was still lost, there remained in him a nostalgic emotional pressure that arose from the happy times he had had with them. This emotional pressure rose out of the herd impulse and it told him that being with your own kind, with other humans, was good. Even the Murtos showed a fondness for the companionship of their own fellows.

Seeing the two men below him, this hunger to be with his own kind became very strong in the jungle man. He wanted to be with humans, to talk to them, to listen to them talk. His only memory of humans at this point was of his father and his mother. They had been kind to him, always. The emotional reasoning in his mind said that all humans would be the same as his parents.

Standing erect on the ledge, he called out, "Hello!"

A clap of thunder from a clear sky would hardly have startled the two men more than this single word. This, plus the sight of the tall, skin-clad giant suddenly appearing on the ledge above them, startled Gnomer so much that he dropped the venison into the fire. With a single motion of his right hand, he snatched the heavy rifle from its resting place.

"Who are you?" Gnomer shouted.

Jongor was already dropping lithely from the ledge to the ground. A smile on his face, the spear grasped in his left hand, his right hand held up and forward, and weaponless, in the ancient human gesture of friendship, he moved toward them.

Whether it was the smile or the hand held up without a weapon that influenced Gnomer, he did not know. The man held his finger on the trigger of the rifle without pulling.

Jongor did not know how close he was to getting killed.

"What do you want here?" Gnomer demanded.

"Just to talk," Jongor said.

His statement was simple truth. However neither of these men were capable of recognizing truth or of believing it when they heard it spoken. Gnomer managed to hold the impulse to pull the trigger of his gun. Hastily snatching up his rifle leaning against the stone wall, Rouse jerked it to his shoulder.

Jongor did not move. He did not flinch, he did not try to run, he did not lift the spear.

"Hold it!" Gnomer shouted at Rouse.

"But he's got a spear!"

"He hasn't tried to use it."

"But he may try—"

"If he does, then will be time enough to shoot him!" Gnomer said. "Take your rifle away from your shoulder!"

"But—"

"I said to take the gun from your shoulder. I meant exactly what I said! Do it!" Gnomer's voice was hard and flat. Very slightly, he shifted the muzzle of his rifle so that instead of pointing at Jongor, it covered his partner, a movement that was not lost on Emil Rouse.

Rouse, protesting, lowered his rifle.

"I'm sorry if I surprised you," Jongor said. He had the impression that something was very wrong here. Had he done something wrong? "I—I saw your fire and—well, I'm human, too. I thought it would be nice to talk."

Silence greeted this statement. The two men stared at him. The muzzle of Gnomer's rifle had swung back to point at him. The man back against the cliff still held his rifle ready. The silence continued. Jongor grew uncomfortable. Perhaps a further explanation was in order.

"I am Jongor," he said. "I am a friend."

"Oh," Jake Gnomer said. Then he repeated the sound again, "Oh," a grunt that said everything—and nothing. Gnomer's mind was working fast. He was badly startled and did not know what to do. The last creature he had expected to see here in this place was a white man muscled like an Apollo, or like a wrestler, and armed with utterly primitive weapons. He studied the spear, the bow across the back, the feathered tips of the arrows projecting from their quiver, the knife in a skin scabbard in the animal skin that formed a loincloth.

"Who the hell are you?" he blurted out.

The giant continued smiling. "I am Jongor," he patiently repeated. To him, this answered the question.

For Jake Gnomer, this was not an adequate answer. "Where the hell did you come from?"

The wave of Jongor's hand took in all of Lost Land. "From here," he said.

"Well—uh—" Gnomer said. He looked upward, his eyes searching along the ledges that led upward.

"I am alone," Jongor said, interpreting the upward look.

"How do we know that?" Emil Rouse demanded.

The question surprised the jungle man. Didn't they

know he was telling the truth? He looked at Rouse. "You know it because I said it," he answered. Something in his tone of voice made Rouse clutch his rifle tighter.

"Well—uh—sit down," Jake Gnomer said. He put sympathy into his voice. "You startled us. Sit down and have a chunk of venison. Tell us about yourself, how you happen to be here alone, how you got here, and so on."

Jongor refused the meat. He was not hungry. Eating when he was not hungry was something he simply did not do. However, he sat down. Squatting on his heels, he told them the story of his life as he knew it, how he had been born here, how his parents had been killed by the pterodactyls, and how he had lived here alone after the death of his parents. He did not mention Ann or Alan Hunter but he was not aware of this oversight. He simply did not remember them.

"Well, whatta you know?" Emil Rouse said, over and over again as he listened. Jake Gnomer listened carefully but said very little.

"So you have lived here all your life?" Gnomer finally questioned.

"Yes," Jongor answered.

"And you know nothing of the rest of the world?"

"Only what my mommy and daddy told me about it," Jongor answered. His voice had in it the high tones of a child when he spoke of his parents—but they were the voice tones of a sad child.

"Um?" Gnomer said. "Then you must know this valley pretty well?"

"Fairly well," Jongor answered.

"Have you been everywhere in it?"

"No."

"Why not?"

"I guess mostly because it's so big that I haven't got around to seeing all of it as yet," Jongor explained. "Also there are places here—" He shook his head at his own thought. "Well, there are places here it is best to stay away from!"

"If you ask my opinion, it's damned good sense to stay away from the whole blasted place!" Emil Rouse spoke.

"No one asked your opinion, Emil," Jake Gnomer answered. Rouse lapsed into quick silence. The burly man turned his attention back to Jongor. "Did you ever hear of an old ruined city where some missing links live?"

"*Missing links?*" Jongor questioned. "I do not understand these words?"

"Some scientists speculate that maybe there is a missing link between the animal and the human world," Gnomer explained. "These missing links might look a lot like big monkeys. They might also have tails—"

"Oh, you mean the Murtos," Jongor said. A fleeting expression of anger crossed his face and was gone almost as soon as it appeared. "Yes, I know how to find the old Murto city. It is a smelly place."

As he was speaking, the expression on Gnomer's face showed suddenly deepening interest.

"Did you hear what he said, Jake?" Rouse questioned. "He said—"

"I know what he said," Gnomer answered. Again he turned to Jongor. "Could you show us how to reach this old Murto city?"

"I suppose I could." A frown crossed the face of the jungle man. "But why do you want to go there?"

"Because—" Rouse began.

"Because we are scientists," Gnomer interrupted his companion. "We were sent here by the International Society for Human Progress. Did you ever hear of this group?"

"No," Jongor said.

"It's a big outfit," Gnomer continued. He was quite certain that Jongor had never heard of this group. No such group existed. Gnomer had invented it to lend an air of authority to his presence here. "The Society has heard rumors of these missing links that you call the Murtos and has sent us to investigate them to find out if they really are the long-lost missing links between the human and the animal worlds.

In startled surprise, Emil Rouse stared at his companion. Gnomer's voice was suave and sounded guileless.

"Scientists?" Jongor asked. "I do not believe I know the meaning of this word either."

"Scientists are people who devote their lives to solving

the problems of the world, who explore the unknown, who search out new facts of nature and give them to the world so that all may benefit from them."

"I do not believe I have ever met any people like this," Jongor said.

"Of course you have!" Gnomer answered. "From what you have told me of them, your parents were scientists. When they tried to fly across this vast valley, they were certainly exploring a new world."

"Oh!" Jongor said. The man's words sounded good. They seemed brave and honest and truthful. The only thing wrong with the words was that he did not believe them. There was a feeling of insincerity about them, of deceit, and of doubt. The Murtos often lied. Was this man also lying? Jongor did not know. All he knew was that he had come here seeking companionship, friendship, someone to talk to.

Gnomer smiled at him. The smile was perhaps the friendliest expression the jungle man had ever seen. The only thing wrong with the smile was that it reminded Jongor of the Murto called Great Orbo. He knew Great Orbo to be a liar. Was this man also a liar?

"We want you to guide us to this old ruined city," Gnomer continued.

Jongor was silent.

"We will pay you well," Gnomer continued.

"Pay me with what?" Jongor asked. Sudden sharp surprise was in his voice.

"Why—why—we will pay you with—with—with whatever you want," Gnomer answered. Worry was in his voice. He had not expected this question. "Anyhow, this won't be much work for you. All you have to do is guide us through country you already know well to the city of the Murtos. You ought to do this without pay, just as a favor."

Jongor made up his mind about this man. The fellow was lying. He shook his head.

"No, I will not guide you to the city of the Murtos," he said.

Gnomer shifted the rifle. Jongor found himself looking into its muzzle.

The jungle man knew guns. His father had owned one here in this land. However his father's rifle had long ago become useless due to a lack of ammunition. For this reason, his father had turned to bows and to spears. However, Jongor knew what guns could do to people. Surprised and shocked, he stared at this one. Why was this man threatening him? He had done nothing wrong.

"Get your hands above your head!" Gnomer snapped. "No, don't reach for that spear or that knife! I'll kill you if you do."

"But you said you were scientists. You said scientists were supposed to help people—" Jongor protested.

"It don't matter what I said. Get your hands above your head, stand up, and turn around. If you make a wrong move, or try to grab the spear or knife, I'll blow your guts out through your backbone."

Silently, letting the spear fall beside him, Jongor rose to his feet. The knife was jerked from his belt. From behind, the bow was lifted over his head and the arrows were jerked from the quiver.

The jungle man attempted no resistance. He did not begin to understand the reasons behind this man's incomprehensible actions. Were all men like this? Was this the way men treated their friends?

Somewhere inside him he was aware of a feeling that all men did not act as Gnómer was acting.

He felt his hands jerked behind his back and tied there.

"Now you will guide us to the city of the Murtos!" the burly man said, triumph in his voice.

Jongor turned to face this man. In spite of the fact that Jongor was weaponless and his hands were tied behind his back, Gnomer involuntarily took a step away from him as he turned.

"Don't you start anything—" the burly man began.

"I—I just don't understand," Jongor answered.

"What is it you don't get?"

"Well, everything. Why you should point a gun at me. Why you should take my weapons. Why you should want me to guide you to the Murto city—"

Now, for the first time, Gnomer realized there was

something wrong with this man. What it was, the burly man did not know, but it seemed to him that this jungle giant had the mind of a child.

"Are you looking for the Murto gold and diamonds that are in the treasure vaults of this old city?" Jongor continued, while Gnomer stared at him.

Gnomer's stare grew more intense when Jongor asked this question. Rouse became quite excited.

"Jake, did you hear what he said?" Rouse demanded.

"I heard him," Gnomer answered.

"About the gold and the diamonds—" Rouse continued.

"I said I heard him," Gnomer said. He turned to Jongor. "What is this crazy talk about gold and diamonds?"

"It is not crazy talk. I have been in the storage vaults. I have seen the diamonds stored in wicker baskets that are so old they have mostly rotted away and let the gems spill out on the floor. I have seen the little gold bars, each one as heavy as a strong Murto could carry, stacked as high as my head."

"Holy hell!" Gnomer said. "How did all of this treasure get there."

"Long, long ago this Murto city was a mining town. Great ships came regularly and took away the gold and the diamonds. Then something happened to the homeland from which the ships came. They came no more. However, for a very long time after this, the Murtos continued mining, thinking that some day the ships would come again. Then the young Murtos decided they would work no more in the mines. They revolted and the mining stopped. Having little left to do, the Murtos started to go downhill. All of this happened a long, long time ago, many tens of thousands of years in the past," Jongor explained.

"How do you know about this?"

"The Murtos told me. I speak their tongue."

"Why—" Rouse could not be restrained from speaking. "Why didn't you grab this off for yourself? What I mean, man, is that you would have been rich! Why didn't you grab it?"

Jongor stared at this man, then slowly shook his head. "To me the diamonds were pretty stones, fit for nothing. The gold was only a heavy yellow metal that was too soft for arrow heads or knives. Why should I wear myself out carrying it from one place to another?"

Their mouths hanging open, the two men stared at him. "Is he out of his head, Jake? Do you think he has taken leave of his senses—or didn't he have any sense to begin with?"

"I don't know," Gnomer answered slowly. "Something is wrong with him, that's for sure, but what it is I don't know. And that's not important. The important thing is whether or not this gold and these diamonds are still there? Are they there, Jongor?"

"So far as I know, they are," Jongor answered. "The Murtos are too lazy to move them. No one else knows where they are. Are they the reason you are seeking the lost city of the Murtos?"

"Well, they weren't the reason, but now that we know about them, they are an additional reason for going there. We'll start first thing in the morning. And don't get any ideas that you can slip away during the night. If you try it—" He patted his rifle.

Jongor was silent.

Gnomer looked at Rouse. "You lost the maps but fate has brought us a better one."

"I am not a map," Jongor said.

"Of course you're not," Gnomer answered. "But you'll do until we find a better one."

Anger rose in the jungle man. These men had tricked him. Now they were laughing at him. The first of his own kind he had ever met had turned out to be rats!

Or were these the first of his kind he had ever met?

As this question came into his mind, an image came flickering into sight, a picture of a laughing woman. The image was gone before he could grasp its meaning. Also, why did these two men seem to think there was something wrong with him? He was Jongor and he was all right!

The two men asked him dozens of questions about

the city of the Murtos, where it was located and how best to reach it. With dignity, he answered their questions.

All the time he talked to them, anger was building up inside him. It was helpless anger, and he knew it. But what could he do about it? The helpless feeling gave him the impression that he was a child. He could do nothing about this impression either.

He was a giant chained by impressions resulting from damage done to his brain—a helpless giant, a giant who felt like a child, thought like a child, and who had the heart of a child.

A child lost in the strange land of his own memory!

Chapter IV

Among the Murtos

In the silence of the night, while the Murtos snored around her, Ann Hunter worked desperately with the rawhide ropes that bound her wrists behind her back. Near her, she was aware that Alan was awake and was working too, as silently and as desperately as she was. Several yards away from them but near the great fire the Murtos had built, Calazao snored like some rusty jet engine.

The Murtos themselves were restless sleepers. To them, the night was a traditional time of danger. Each one lay as near the fire as he could get without taking the risk of burning his furry hide. Or his even more precious tail! Guards had been posted away from the fire. They were apprehensive and alert. Off somewhere in the darkness a lion growled. At the sound, a frightened monkey chittered in the tree tops.

At the sound of the lion, the Murtos stirred, each making certain that his spear and his club were handy; then they slipped back into uneasy sleep. On the far side of the fire, Great Orbo, their leader, dozed against a tree trunk. Somewhere on the other side of the fire away from Orbo, Umber slept uneasily.

The Murtos were frightened not only of the animals that hunted by night but also by the ghosts that they

considered came alive as soon as night came, by the
phantoms that they believed existed in the darkness.
That these phantoms were often the products of their
own imaginations they did not understand.

Ann and Alan Hunter lay a little apart from the Murtos. Kego, who had held the skin ropes by which their
hands had been tied, was sound asleep near them. Kego
was not concerned about the possibility that his captives
might escape. To flee into the darkness was to run to certain death in Kego's opinion. Better to sleep by the fire
and stay alive than to run into the darkness and become
lion food!

Ann Hunter's hope was that she could get her hands
free, then free her brother's hands, then the two of them
could slip away into the jungle where they would be
free. Free in Lost Land where death lurked behind every
bush, where it waited at every waterhole, where it lay
hidden on the tall cliffs.

Better the dangers of Lost Land then captivity by the
Murtos, Ann felt. Suddenly she was aware of a whisper
near her. Thinking this whisper came from Jongor, her
heart leaped into her throat. Then the whisper came
again.

"Sis!"

Now she knew the whisper had come from her
brother. She answered him.

"I've got my hands free," Alan whispered.

Ann felt her pulse jump at his words. Now she became
aware that Alan was moving, that he was sliding slowly
across the ground, coming nearer and nearer to her. She
turned on her side so he could reach her wrists, then felt
his fingers begin to explore the knots there.

"This stuff is slippery and the knot is hard," Alan whispered. "But lie still and give me time."

She lay without moving. Somewhere out toward the
edge of the firelight, Umber awakened. Apparently
awakening in a nightmare, Umber stumbled toward
them. Ann Hunter held her breath.

"Get away from her!" Umber snarled at Alan. He
kicked at the youth. Ann saw that Alan had rolled away
from her. "Don't come near her again!"

"He's my brother and he can come as close to me as he wants," Ann said quickly, in the Murto language.

"Shhh, Sis," Alan said, in English. "Don't provoke the damned fool!"

"What is this strange talk?" Umber demanded. "What did he say about me?"

"He said you are the greatest Murto who ever lived and that you will be king soon!" Ann answered.

"Umph!" Umber said. He suspected this female was not telling the truth but he was pleased just the same. "What else did he say?"

"He said we should always do as you tell us," Ann continued. "He said that when you are king, you will be our friend."

"Good," Umber said. Satisfaction sounded in his voice. Even if this female was lying, her lies were good to hear. He decided that she pleased him and he wanted her to please him even more. Dropping to his knees beside her, his hands sought her face as he tried to turn it toward him.

Ann Hunter's first startled thought was that this monkey-man was trying to kiss her. An instant later, she remembered that the Murtos had never discovered kissing, that among them affection was shown by rubbing noses. The young woman felt the hot breath of the Murto on her face, felt his nose gently touching her. A shock wave of panic rolled through her.

Ann Hunter wanted to scream but knew that a scream would attract the attention of the other Murtos. She did not know what the other Murtos would do if they saw this Murto rubbing noses with her. Perhaps they would want to rub noses with her too! Also, if she cried out, Kego would be certain to awaken. He might find out that Alan had succeeded in freeing his hands from the skin ropes. If this was discovered, their chance of escape would be gone forever!

The young woman stifled the impulse to scream.

"You pretty thing!" Umber grunted.

"You dirty beast!" Ann answered, in English.

"What do those words mean?"

"They describe how strong you are," Ann said, in Murto.

"Ah!"

She could hear the purr of satisfaction in Umber's voice. He was very pleased with this female. Perhaps, if he rubbed noses with her again—

Again she felt his breath on her face, hotter now than before, and again she felt him touch her nose. Pressure too great to be held down rose within her. It came exploding to the surface, in the form of an ear-splitting scream.

The sleeping Murtos instantly awakened. Great Orbo, grasping his heavy club in both hands, came bounding from the other side of the fire. Kego awakened, to jerk at the leather ropes. Calazao's snores went into silence. Looking around for the enemy that had disturbed his rest, he grasped his axe and lumbered to his feet.

"What's going on here?" Great Orbo shouted. "Why is this female screaming? You, Umber, what are you doing so close to her?"

"She is having a bad dream and I am trying to get her to shut up!" Umber answered. Seeing the club in his chief's hand, Umber got quickly to his feet and backed away.

"Were you having a bad dream?" Orbo asked Ann.

"Yes," the frightened young woman said. It was better to accept Umber's explanation than to tell the truth. "Sometimes I have these dreams and I awaken screaming. Now go back to sleep, all of you. I'll try not to have another nightmare."

To her surprise, and to her great relief, the Murtos accepted her suggestion. Muttering, Orbo returned to the far side of the fire. Umber went back to the edge of the shadows. Kego laid back down. Eventually the whole camp was quiet and Calazao was snoring again.

"Be quiet, Sis," Alan whispered, near her.

Ann Hunter did not move a muscle as she felt Alan's fingers tugging at the tough cords that bound her wrists together. She heard him grunt softly, with satisfaction— and then her hands were free. Cautiously and slowly, she drew them to the front of her body, quietly rubbing the wrists to restore circulation.

"Sis, we're going to crawl like snakes until we're out of the light of the fire—" Alan said. Mutely, she nodded. Alan's movement was so slow it seemed to be no motion at all but she knew he was crawling toward the edge of the jungle. She also knew he hesitated long enough to grasp a spear lying on the ground beside a sleeping Murto and to pull it along with him.

Minutes later they were in the darkness and were standing up and hugging each other.

Somewhere in the jungle near them, a restless sentry cleared his throat. They froze at the sound.

"We have to find our way around him," Alan said. "Stay close to me!"

"You don't have to tell me to—to do—that—" the frightened young woman stuttered. "I'll follow you like a shadow."

She did exactly this, keeping one hand touching his back, moving with him every time he moved.

When the sentry coughed again, he was well behind them. Then they moved much faster. Only when the light of the Murto fire could no longer be seen did they dare stop to catch their breaths.

"I never would have believed it could happen!" Ann gasped, breathing heavily. "But we did it, thanks to you. We got away! We're free!"

"We come of a breed of people who never learned how to quit," Alan answered. "Our next job is to find Jongor. I was dead certain he would be somewhere around the Murto camp tonight, trying to rescue us."

"So was I!"

"What's bugging me is why he hasn't showed."

"Maybe he is around here somehwere in the dark jungle," Ann said, sudden eagerness in her voice. "Maybe he has been waiting for a chance to help us get free! Maybe he doesn't even know we have escaped. In this dark place, it's hard to be certain about anything."

"We'll go as far as we can during the night," Alan decided. "Tomorrow he will either find us or we will find him. Come on, Sis."

"I'll bet he finds us," Ann said. "Without him—" She did not finish what she had on her mind. She knew as well as Alan did that getting out of Lost Land without Jongor to help them would be a difficult to impossible task.

Without Jongor, just staying alive in this deadly land would be difficult.

"Let's put distance between us and those Murtos," Alan said.

They moved quietly through the dark jungle. In the trees above them, a night bird twittered. In the far distance, from the direction of the Murto camp, a lion roared.

"I hope he decides to have Murto for dinner," Alan said. "If he comes toward us, we go up the trees. Remember that, Sis. If the lion comes, up a tree!"

"You don't have to tell me to climb a tree," Ann answered. "I may have to outrun a lion, but at least I don't have to rub noses with Umber!"

Although neither knew it, their escape from the Murto camp had not been unseen. As they slipped into the darkness, a monkey-man quietly followed them—Umber.

Umber had been so pleased by the nose rubbing that he had been unable to go back to sleep. Something about nose rubbing with this strange female excited him greatly.

He watched Ann and Alan begin their stealthy crawl to the edge of the firelight. His first thought was to alarm the camp and help recapture them. Great Orbo would forgive him his past sins and would probably reward him with an extra wife or two for capturing two escaping captives.

Following the first thought was a second idea. Umber let them escape, then, heavy club in hand, he followed them. In the darkness one blow with the club would knock the brains out of the head of the female's brother.

After that, he could rub noses with the female as much as he wanted!

Ann and Alan moved furtively through the darkness. A half moon was rising now. Under its rays, Lost Land was a fantastically beautiful place, a fairyland of mingled light and shadow. Neither had eyes for the beauty of the place at the moment. Each knew they were not safe, and probably never would be safe, in this place. Off to their left, Ann heard a rustle of sound. She pretended not to hear it. Once or twice, behind them, she thought she heard the sound of heavy footsteps. She ignored these too. "It's my nerves," she told herself. "I'm tired—and I'm imagining things!" There was comfort in the thought that the real sounds she heard from time to time were only imaginary—but not much comfort.

Resolutely, the spear always ready in his hand, Alan went forward. If he heard suspicious sounds, he said nothing about them. For this, she was grateful to him. From the distance came the full-throated roar of a lion. To this sound, neither gave any thought. A lion that roared was not hunting for his dinner. However the lion's roar served to remind them of the dangers here. Each knew they might survive without Jongor but each also knew that their best chance of staying alive in this playground of hell was to find the jungle man. He knew how to stay alive here!

Behind them, Ann was again aware of footsteps.

"Alan, we're being followed!" she whispered.

Spear ready, Alan turned to the rear. A night wind was moving through the trees. Shadows in dark patches lay everywhere. And in any dark patch anything could be lurking. Alan listened. "I don't hear anything," he said at last.

"I don't either, now," Ann answered. "But—"

"There are all kinds of little sounds in this jungle at night," Alan said. "Sometimes our imagination—"

"I know," Ann agreed hurriedly.

"Maybe you heard an animal. A deer—"

"It didn't sound like a deer!" Ann could hear her own heart beating as she listened.

"Come on," Alan said.

A grove of trees was ahead of them. Alan went directly into it, into the darkness there. Ann tried to protest. He ignored her words. When he stopped, she bumped into him. "Here, I'll give you a hand up," he said.

"What—"

"You're going up this tree."

She tried to protest but again he ignored her. Up

above, she could vaguely see the lowest limb of a tall tree. Alan boosted her up, she caught the limb, threw a leg over it, and drew herself up on it.

"Go as high as you can," Alan told her.

"You're coming too?" she questioned. "Here! Reach up and catch my hand. I'll pull you up."

"I'm going to stay down here for a while," Alan answered. "You get yourself securely settled up there."

"But—"

"Shhh!"

She was silent.

"What you were hearing back behind us was not your imagination," Alan said. "Something is following us! I'm going to wait here against the trunk of the tree."

"But, Alan!"

"*Shhh!*"

Now her ears caught a sound that was coming from the edge of the grove where they had entered. It was not the thump of footsteps; it was the rustle of a body brushing lightly against foliage.

"Can you see anything?" Alan whispered to her, from the base of the tree.

"No," she answered.

Ann Hunter crouched in the tree. A soft breeze moved through the leaves. Other than the rustling whisper of the wind there was no sound. What was following them in the jungle night? Desperately she hoped it might be Jongor but she knew it was not the jungle man. Jongor would recognize them, would call out to them, and would come to them. This thing followed them! Every sense alert, she listened. The soft, almost undistinguishable sounds of stealthy movement came to her ears from the darkness in the grove. She repressed the impulse to scream.

What was down there? She did not know. She wanted to call out to Alan, to warn him but she knew that any sound she made would only call their position to the attention of whatever was down there. Was she really hearing the sounds? She told herself that she was sensing them with some form of perception higher than her ears, with a kind of psychic sense, doing this in an effort to ease the tension mounting sky-high in her. This did not produce the desired result. It made no difference whether she was hearing the sounds or was sensing them, the sounds still existed and they meant that something was coming cautiously through the trees toward them.

She strained her eyes trying to see. Patches of moonlight filtered through gaps in the leaves of the trees. She saw something dark, black, and furry start to move into a patch of moonlight, then, as if it was aware that it had been seen, move hastily out of sight.

Again she heard the soft scratch of branches as some heavy body moved through them. She tried to watch the patches of moonlight down below. Whatever was down there was now evading the light from the moon.

The scratching sounds continued past the tree. She took a deep breath that was pure relief. Whatever it was that had been following them had failed to see them and had gone past them! There was joy in this thought.

Then she heard it turn back! Immediately thereafter a heavy thud sounded at the foot of the tree, such a thud as might have come from a club striking a resisting object.

"Uh!" a voice cried out in pain.

This was a voice she recognized! "Alan!" she cried out. "Are you hurt?"

She started down the tree, then stopped quickly as another thump came from below. This time a heavy grunt followed the sound of some weapon landing. Alan had a spear, she knew, but a spear made little sound as the point struck home. However, if Alan had struck with the spear shaft instead of with the point, a sound such as she had heard might have resulted from the blow.

The heavy grunt that came after the thump could have come from whatever it was that had been following them! The grunt told her nothing of the identity of this creature.

Instantly there followed another thump, then from under the tree came the sound of violent battle. Down there a club struck at a spear and the spear in turn lunged for the club-holder, lunged and missed. Down there in the darkness, Alan Hunter cried out in sudden pain.

Ann Hunter hesitated for only a second, then started down the tree. No matter what happened to her, she intended to go down there into that darkness and help her brother.

Before she reached the lowest limb, the sounds of struggle ended in another thud. Instantly she stopped moving down the tree. Below was silence. She started to cry out, then stopped the sound before it was uttered. With bated breath she stood on the lowest limb trying to see what had happened in the darkness below.

Down there was only silence. The whole grove was silent. It was as if the trees had been shocked by some tragedy that had taken place within the grove, an event that had silenced even the leafy whisperings. A cloud moved across the face of the moon.

With the moon gone, the space on the ground around the base of the tree became very dark. In that darkness, Ann Hunter could hear someone—or some *thing!*—breathing heavily. She did not know what it was. The moon stayed behind its cloud and the darkness continued. So did the silence.

"Alan?" Ann whispered, in desperation.

When there was no answer, she instantly knew that she should not have called out. She had given away the fact that she was in the tree!

Down below was movement. She felt a slight movement in the trunk of the tree as something touched it. Reaching above, she caught the next branch and pulled herself up on it. There she waited.

A grunt below told her that something down there had reached upward and had caught the lowest limb. She called out again, sharper now. "Alan?"

There was no answer. Perhaps her brother had been hurt and could not speak. Did this account for his silence?

The cloud slipped away from the face of the moon and she saw what was directly below her on the tree. Below her—and climbing upward.

It was a Murto—Umber.

Chapter V

An Old Friend from the Swamp

"Move out," Gnomer said. "If you try to escape, or if you guide us anywhere except to the old city of the Murtos, if you try to trick us—" He patted the stock of his rifle.

"Why should I try to trick you?" Jongor answered. "It doesn't matter to me where I take you."

"Get going," Gnomer said.

Moving westward, Jongor walked away from the overhanging ledge where he had spent the night with the two men who had captured him. He did not look back but the sounds behind him told him they were following him. To him, this did not matter. Nothing mattered to him, except the image of a woman that now and again appeared in his mind but which always flitted away like an elusive butterfly before he could catch it.

Following behind him, he knew that Gnomer and Rouse were watching him very closely. He also knew they would shoot him if he tried to escape.

Picking his way through the jungle, skirting stretches of open water, wading through reedy swamps, Jongor heard Gnomer and Rouse cursing behind him.

"Slow down, damn you!" Rouse shouted at him.

Jongor slowed down. It did not matter to him how fast he went, or how slow.

At noon, they stopped and made a small fire, which they used to roast chunks of venison. They offered meat to Jongor, but he refused it, saying he was not hungry yet.

"Do you eat only when you're hungry?" Rouse asked.

"Yes," Jongor said. He tried to talk to Rouse, trying to find out from him why the two men wanted to reach the old city of the Murtos but Gnomer cut into the conversation.

"Maybe we just want to get rich," Gnomer said. "From what you have told us, the Murtos were once a colony of miners. For generations, they piled up gold and diamonds in their forgotten city—"

"But you learned about this from me," Jongor pointed out. "Before you found out about the gold and the diamonds, you had a reason for trying to find the old city. What was it?"

"Scientists don't need any reason except that they want to find something that is lost or hidden," Gnomer said.

"Oh," Jongor said. The man's words seemed plausible and reasonable.

"Of course, now that we see a chance to get rich too, we're even more eager," Gnomer continued.

Jongor stared at the burly man. "What is *rich?*" he asked. "What does it mean. What do you do when you are rich that you do not do when you are poor? I do not understand." Bewilderment showed in his eyes.

Glancing at his partner, Gnomer made a circling motion with his forefinger pointed at his forehead. Then he tried to explain to this simple child of the jungle the meaning of being rich.

"It's having a lot of money," the burly man said. "It's having a big house in New York City, another house in Connecticut, another house in London, and a house on the Mediterranean. It's having a boat big enough to sail around the world and a private jet plane that can fly anywhere. Being rich is having cars and servants and your name in the paper."

Uncomprehendingly, the jungle man stared at Gnomer. "Can you live in all of those houses at once?" he asked.

"Well, no—" Gnomer admitted.

"Then why don't you give them to people who need them?" Jongor asked.

Open-mouthed, the burly man stared at him. "You *must* be crazy!" Gnomer exploded.

"What is *crazy?*" Jongor asked.

"Oh, shut up!" Gnomer snapped at him. "Get up and get going. But if you ever think of escaping, remember *this*." Again he patted the stock of his rifle.

"If I tried to escape, would I be crazy?" the jungle man asked.

"You sure as hell would!" Gnomer replied.

Jongor shrugged. "But why did you come here seeking the city of the Murtos?" he persisted.

"If you think I'm going to tell you that, then you really are crazy," the burly man said. "Now shut up and move out."

Rising to his feet, Jongor obeyed.

Now the route lay closer to the mountains. Often steep climbs had to made. Always the two men thought Jongor was deliberately taking the hard way.

"He's just trying to wear us out!" Rouse said, repeatedly.

Climbing a slope, the jungle man slipped. He fell backward into Rouse. When he was slow rising, Rouse kicked him in the bottom. As Jongor rose to his feet and looked at him, Rouse backed hastily away, lifting his rifle.

"Don't shoot him before we reach the Murto city," Gnomer said hastily.

"Then tell him not to look at me like that!" Rouse said, taking another step away.

After Jongor had risen to his feet and had turned, his eyes had been filled with a blazing light.

"Don't kick me again!" he said.

"If I do, what'll you do about it?" Rouse challenged, fingering his rifle.

"I'll break your neck," Jongor said. He turned away. Rouse lifted his rifle.

"Cut it out!" Gnomer snarled at him.

"But he threatened me—"

"So would I, if you kicked me in the bottom when I

was down," Gnomer answered. He nodded toward Jongor, who was already climbing the slope ahead. "Don't let him get too far ahead. He might decide to slip over the top of the rise and run away."

Rouse moved to place himself within easy rifle range of the jungle man.

Perhaps it was the kick, which made him furious, that also made Jongor realize that these men meant to kill him as soon as he had showed them the city of the Murtos. Gnomer's words had confirmed the impression. In his mind, Jongor began to form plans to escape. He looked often at the crystal in the bracelet he wore on his left arm, but during the remainder of the day he found no excuse to take a path that led near the swamps. That night they tied his hands and his legs before they slept. The next day they went forward through rolling hills that had a great swamp to the left.

"It would be easier walking near the water," Rouse pointed out.

Silently, Jongor agreed. As they skirted the edges of the swamp, he watched the water, looking always for a number of small birds perched on what looked to be a small, rocky island.

In mid-afternoon, Gnomer shot a deer. They made camp, lit a small fire, and roasted steaks near the edge of the water. Hungry now, Jongor ate raw meat with relish.

"Don't you want it cooked?" Rouse asked.

"Why spoil good meat by sticking it into a fire?" Jongor asked. While the two men were eating, he squatted on his heels and watched the swamp out of the corner of his eyes. Out there was a small island above which small birds were catching gnats in the evening sun. He concentrated his attention on the crystal on his wrist. Did the island begin to move? He was not certain.

Night began to fall over Lost Land. Somewhere in the vast swamp a bullfrog began to croak, talking out there in a deep bass voice about some mythical *jug-of-rum* that has been standard frog-talk since the world began.

By the fire, the two men cuddled their rifles and talked in low voices. Jongor made no effort to listen to them. He was concentrating his attention on the crystal. Out of the corner of his eyes he was watching the island.

The little birds had flitted away to the reeds where they spent the night. The island was causing a slight wake on the water. A second, much smaller island had appeared now. It moved toward the swamp reeds too.

"What are you thinking about?" Gnomer suddenly asked him.

Jongor shrugged the question away. "Nothing," he answered. "When we get to the city of the Murtos, what will you do with me?"

It was Gnomer's turn to shrug. "We'll turn you loose," the burly man said. His manner was evasive. Jongor was aware that afterwards Gnomer was watching him very closely. He pretended indifference, not even looking at the bracelet on his left wrist. Out of the corner of his eyes, he watched the small island. It had turned away from the reeds and was now moving directly toward the shore of the swamp in front of the fire.

Suck-splash!

The small island suddenly came out of the water. It was revealed now as the head of something that looked like a huge snake that had thrust itself partly out of the water. In the dusk, eyes looked toward the shore.

The two men leaped to their feet. "What the hell is that?" Gnomer shouted.

Jongor did not move. His entire attention was now concentrated on the crystal.

This crystal was a very unusual stone. Gray in color, veins of glowing light were now visible in it. The stone itself was set in a dull yellow metal. If either Gnomer or Rouse had examined the setting, they would have become wildly excited. The setting was soft yellow gold in an almost pure state.

As Jongor concentrated his full attention on the crystal, the veins of light glowed stronger.

Down at the edge of the swamp, the long neck projected from the water. The snake head twisted and turned as if it was trying to smell an odor or perhaps pick up a vibration from the air. The eyes were also trying to see.

Jongor stared at the crystal.

"Come, little one," he whispered, over and over again. "Come, little one."

The eyes concentrated their gaze in his direction but the head did not move.

"Here I am, little one," Jongor repeated.

The head shook itself in the air. The eyes concentrated on the small blaze. The head drew back.

"The fire will not burn you, little one," Jongor said. "You need not fear it. I will protect you from it. Come to me, little one."

"Look at him!" Rouse screamed, pointing to the jungle man. "He's talking to that damned thing! He's calling it up here!" Wild fear was in the man's voice. "You!" His rifle covered Jongor.

The jungle man did not even look up.

"Stop it!" Gnomer knocked the rifle barrel aside.

"But I tell you—"

"Didn't you ever try that on a cue ball, didn't you ever try to talk a horse home? That's all he's doing!"

"Come ashore, little one," Jongor said.

In the swamp, something snorted in reply. A ripple spread out from the neck as the head started to move. An instant later, both the ripple and the bigger island suddenly enlarged from the water.

"Is—is that a submarine?" Rouse gasped.

"Don't be stupid!" Gnomer answered. "There can't be a submarine in these swamps! There just can't!"

The submarine that could not exist came ashore. From both sides it threw up heavy waves, then as the body appeared, feet could be seen. As these feet lifted themselves from the muddy bottom of the lake the sounds were similar to those of a battery of heavy pumps in operation, pumps that were sucking a mixture of mud and water.

The thing from the swamp crashed through the low trees growing at the edge of the water and stood there, a creature out of Earth's long-gone past. The neck was similar to that of a gigantic snake. The eyes were like saucers. The eyes watched the little fire. The neck twisted and turned. Sniffing and snorting, it reached toward the fire, then hastily drew back from the little blaze.

"A—a—a dinosaur!" Gnomer gasped, as he recognized the creature that had come up from the swamp. He did not recognize the monster as being one of the vegetation-eating dinosaurs, one of the huge lumbering creatures that usually fed from lakes or from streams in Earth's long-gone past, feeding in this way because the vast bulk of the body needed support from water. Not that these dinosaurs could not walk on land—they certainly could, for long distances—but they were generally more comfortable in the water.

There were other dinosaurs in Lost Land, the meat-eaters, the terrible thunder lizards, creatures that could gobble down a whole deer at a single gulp.

Although dinosaurs, or "dinos," as he called them, had been familiar to Jongor since his childhood, neither Gnomer nor Rouse had ever seen such a creature. Nor had they had any knowledge that such monsters existed.

Forgetting Jongor, they stared at the dripping dinosaur as it came up from the swamp. Their rifles were ready but at this moment the very sight of the swamp monster froze them where they stood.

"Come on, little one," Jongor whispered softly.

Twisting its long neck, the gigantic beast seemed to be trying to pick up a familiar smell. It did not like the sight of the little blaze. Then it began to moan, a low wailing sound that had in it hair-raising tones. Keeping a close watch on the fire, it began to move.

"Jake!" Rouse gulped. "Jake!"

Both men threw up their rifles. Both fired at the same split second. The sharp, spiteful crack of the weapons rang out through Lost Land.

The dinosaur snorted. It moved forward. The long neck snaked toward the two men.

"You might as well shoot an elephant with a pop-gun!" Rouse exploded. He was running as he spoke.

Gnomer had stronger nerves, a stouter courage. He faced the movement of the swamp monster. The rifle in his hands rang out again. He was aiming at the head, a hard shot. He could not tell whether or not he hit his target. However, one thing was obvious—the long neck was reaching toward him.

At this point, Gnomer's nerves broke. Turning, he followed his companion.

Each ran a short distance. Finding they were not being followed, they stopped. Looking back, they saw the mighty creature reach the spot where they had been standing only seconds before.

Jongor was rising to his feet. The dinosaur was lumbering toward him. He was making no effort to escape.

"Get out of there, fast!" Gnomer shouted. "That thing will trample you into the ground!"

Jongor did not move. Moving warily around the little fire, the dinosaur stopped beside him. The long neck extended down toward him.

"It's going to eat him alive!" Rouse gulped.

Very gently, Jongor patted the dinosaur on the nose. Like a cat rubbing its head against the legs of a beloved master, the great beast rubbed its head against his body. Like a cowboy mounting a horse, the jungle man swung one leg over its neck. Settling himself in place there, he looked in the gathering dusk for the two men.

"He's going to ride that thing!" Rouse whispered.

"But he can't be riding it!" Gnomer protested. "It's just not possible! He can't—"

Looking in the dusk, Jongor finally spotted Gnomer and Rouse. His hand flung up to point at them.

"After them, little one!" Jongor's voice lifted. "Trample them into the dirt! They tried to kill you! Show them how it feels to be walked on by a mountain!"

In response, the dinosaur moaned. Still carefully avoiding the fire, it moved toward the two men!

"Faster, thou cousin of the snake! Move quickly, brother of the crocodile!" Jongor shouted.

Again the dinosaur moaned.

"Catch them, little one!" the jungle man shouted. "Show them who is really boss in Lost Land!"

The moan of the dinosaur rang out again in answer.

"You can stay here if you want to, Jake, but I'm heading for a mountain to climb!" Rouse said.

"I'm right with you!" Gnomer answered.

Turning, the two men ran as if chased by devils. Following them came the shouts of Jongor, the moan of the dinosaur, and the thump of heavy feet.

"They tricked me, little one!" Jongor shouted. "When I went to them as a friend, they pointed guns at me! They were going to shoot me!"

In response, the dinosaur moaned louder, a low throbbing sound that spread over the swamp and which echoed back from the mountains.

"Teach them manners, little one!" Jongor shouted.

Eventually, as the darkness increased, Jongor could no longer see the fleeing men. Nor could the dinosaur smell them. When the great beast halted, the jungle man turned it away from the chase.

"You have taught them a lesson, little one. Now we must go in another direction."

Ponderously, the dinosaur turned. It would have headed back to its beloved swamp but Jongor prevented this.

"No, thou brother of the crocodile, you are not going back into the swamp just yet! This way, mighty beast!" With his right hand, he pointed along the trail he had followed in bringing Gnomer and Rouse into Lost Land.

The dinosaur moaned in protest, but it obeyed him. He had no intention of trying to hunt down the two men. If he cornered them on the dinosaur, and they stood and fought—and even rats would eventually turn and fight— a rifle bullet might knock him from his precarious seat just behind the head of the swamp monster. The two men would eventually be certain that he was controlling the great beast and would aim at him instead of at the dinosaur.

He turned the great beast in the other direction. He wanted his weapons, his bow and arrows, his knife and his spear, which Gnomer and Rouse had taken from him.

Trying to survive in Lost Land without weapons was a gamble that only a fool would take!

The great beast moaned softly.

"That way," Jongor told it. "That way!"

The dinosaur turned in the direction indicated.

In Lost Land, nothing got in the way of a dinosaur.

The great beast travelled in the direction it was to go without hindrance from any other animal. The creatures of the night got out of its way!

Seated on its neck behind its head, Jongor found the position so comfortable that he took short naps with perfect safety. As though it sensed its responsibility to him, each time he dozed the great beast moved with extra care.

Morning had arrived before the dinosaur reached the place where Gnomer and Rouse had captured Jongor. The great beast lowered its head to the ground and he slid down. His spear, the great bow, his quiver of arrows, and the knife were in the brush where Gnomer had thrown them. The great bow and the quiver of arrows went back on his back, and the knife went back into the scabbard in the loinskin that belted his middle.

Moaning, the dinosaur nuzzled against him. He scratched its nose. "Are you hungry, little one?" he asked. When he spoke he concentrated his full attention on the crystal.

The dinosaur nodded its head. He put his arms around its neck and hugged the great beast.

"Are you also tired?"

Again the great beast nodded in answer.

"Thank you, little one, for your help," Jongor said. "But for you, I would still be a captive. And that's no good, little one."

The dinosaur moaned softly. So close was the rapport established by the crystal between the animal's mind and Jongor's mind that he could feel its thinking. He rubbed its nose. Happiness which he could feel through the crystal flowed out of it like a tidal wave.

"Go back to your beloved swamp, little one," Jongor said. When the dinosaur hesitated, Jongor hastened to reassure it. "I will be all right, little one. Do not be concerned about me. No, I do not wish to swim in the muddy swamp. The crocodiles run from you but they would not run from me. And I cannot eat weeds. However, you go."

Slowly, reluctantly, the great beast turned. When the mighty hind end was near him, Jongor slapped it affectionately, then watched as the huge animal waddled slowly away. A little later, when it reached the nearest swamp and launched itself like a battleship going down the ways, the jungle man felt through the crystal the joy that surged in the mighty animal.

Then he turned his attention away from the crystal— and forgot about the dinosaur.

He was free again, free to live his own life in his own way in his own land! True, the image of a woman kept moving through his mind like a gray ghost trapped in a fog but he saw no reason why this image should concern him.

What did concern him were the hunger pangs rising in his stomach.

Stringing the great bow, he nocked an arrow on the string, then went into the lowlands to hunt. He found a clear trail that told him a group of Murtos had passed this way recently but he had no wish for an encounter with the monkey-men and he did not follow the trail.

When he had eaten, he decided he would return to the great cave where he had lived with his parents when he had been a child. This was the only home he had ever known. Memories of it, strong in his mind, pulled at him to return to the place where he had known love and happiness.

As he made his way across Lost Land, his keen eyes caught the sight of a human figure on his left, a figure which stumbled as it moved. It did not see him, and he took care to prevent their meeting.

With memories of Gnomer and Rouse strong in his mind, he had no intention of approaching another human being or of allowing a human to get near him.

Later, he saw another human in a tree—a female, he thought. He did not know what a female would be doing up a tree in Lost Land but he had no intention of going close enough to any human to find out.

His recent experiences with his two captors said that humans were bad and were to be avoided. If some female chose to climb a tree, that was her business. He had no intention of going near enough to ask her why she had done it.

Avoiding the female up the tree, he continued his leisurely walk across Lost Land.

Chapter VI

Battle in the Tree

When Ann Hunter saw that Umber was directly below her in the tree, and was climbing upward, her first impulse was to scream. Her second, and much better idea, was to kick downward with her feet. She felt her heels strike Umber's head. Almost knocked out of the tree, the Murto squalled in rage. Ann heard him grab frantically at the trunk of the tree, while he tried to catch himself.

Swearing at her, the Murto started back up the tree. She fled upward, pulling herself up from limb to limb, in a flight that she knew was hopeless. Panic rose in her when she knew she could climb no higher. For a moment, her mad impulse was to jump, and to hope that when she hit the ground, this horror would be ended forever.

She fought this impulse—and conquered it. If die she must, she would die fighting this Murto!

A desperate idea came into her mind. Grasping with both hands the limb directly above her, she waited until Umber was directly below her. Then, holding on with her hands, she swung her body at the Murto, kicking him in the face with all her strength.

This time Umber was jarred loose from his grip on the tree.

Squalling like a devil, the Murto fell. She heard his

body thump from branch to branch as it fell downward. Then she felt her hands begin to slip from their grip. Desperately she tried to grasp the limb tighter. The slippery bark gave her no hold for her hands. She felt her body begin to fall, then she knew she was thumping from limb to limb as she fell, too. Down, down, down, she went. Now and then, for an instant, she managed to catch hold of a limb. Those grasping, failing handholds slowed her fall—and probably saved her life.

She did not hit the ground. Instead, she landed directly on top of Umber. Knocked out by the fall, the Murto was unconscious. His body gave her a cushion and she was only dazed. Stumbling to her feet, she called out a single word.

"Alan! Alan! Where are you, Alan!"

There was no answer. At the moment, her dazed thought was that Alan was dead, that he had been killed by the Murto in the battle that had taken place beneath the tree. Whispering her brother's name, she listened for an answer. The only sounds she heard were the night winds in the trees and the heavy strangled breathing of the monkey-man.

Umber began to twist his body on the ground. His strangling stopped and he began to breathe more regularly, sounds that told her he was about to regain consciousness. Panic rose in her. She began to run. She did not run a dozen steps before she stumbled and fell. As she got to her feet, she heard the monkey-man also getting to his feet. Umber was swearing all the Murto oaths he knew, language that would have made her blush under other circumstances but now it made her run faster than she knew was possible. She bumped into trees—and bounced off of them! Briars caught her legs—and she forced her way through them. Tree roots on top of the ground tripped her—and she got to her feet and ran again. Noises behind her told her that Umber was following her. She did not know whether or not the monkey-men could see in the dark but she knew she could take no chances on Umber's night sight.

Reaching the edge of the grove, she found open country ahead of her—and ran as she had never run before. A grazing deer, startled by her flight, began to flee too, moving in great thumping jumps through the moon-lit night. Farther away, another deer began to run. Or she hoped they were deer. Whatever they were, they were running away.

Something hissed at her from the ground. Instinctively she leaped over the snake that was there. Desperately she hoped the snake would strike Umber if the Murto passed this way.

When she could run no longer, she fell to the ground. Panting for breath, she lay there. Noises were in the night. Somewhere to her right, she could hear Umber. The Murto was barking like a hound on the chase. She wondered if the monkey-man could follow her trail by scent as a dog could! Waiting and listening, she heard Umber pass perhaps a hundred yards to her left. Umber was not running by scent or by sight. It seemed to her that he was going in the general direction he thought she had taken.

When her strength had returned, she got to her feet and began to hurry back to the spot from which she had started. Her object was to find her brother. She was sure he was hurt. She was the one to help him.

It did not occur to her that she was barely able to help herself.

"I've got to find Alan. He has to have help. He may be badly hurt.".

With this in her mind, she hurried in the direction from which she had come. The knowledge that Umber was seeking her and was now somewhere behind her added to her haste with the result that she took a wrong turn without realizing she was doing it.

An hour later, she faced the truth: she was lost. In addition, she was weaponless. Also, clouds were now moving heavily over the face of the moon. With the moon gone, she knew how dark the nights could be in Lost Land.

While a little moonlight remained, she found another tree and climbed it. Adding to her misery, rain began to fall during the night.

Morning sun found her cold and wet—but alive. This was the most she could say for herself, that she was still alive. Every muscle in her body was cramped and filled with aches. She could barely make her way down the tree.

Exercises relieved some of the cramped muscles but exercises did not help her find her trail back to the place where she had last seen Alan. Eventually she had to face the fact that she was hopelessly lost in a land of swamp and forest where everything was an enemy and there were no friends except the trees. In addition, she was ravenously hungry.

She solved this problem by eating the fruits and the berries that Jongor had taught her were edible. The jungle man was constantly in her mind. She was certain that he would find her, in time. When the roar of a lion sent her back up her favorite tree in the midafternoon, she even thought she caught a glimpse of Jongor in the distance. Just a glimpse was all she had of the jungle man, then the figure faded into the jungle, leaving her uncertain whether or not she had actually seen anything.

"I must be seeing things," she told herself. "If what I saw was really Jongor, he would have seen me and would have come to rescue me!"

This was the thought that gave her the courage to keep going. She was certain that Jongor would find her. He was an expert tracker. No matter where she went, he would be able to find her trail and to follow it. However, there was some possibility that a few days might pass before he discovered she was not with the band of Murtos. If this happened, then he might need more time to find where she had escaped from the band. Also the rain had possibly washed out much of her trail, which might delay him further.

But rain or no rain, Murtos or no Murtos, lost trail or no lost trail, in the end Jongor would find her. In her heart, she was certain of this.

Coming down from the tree, she went to the spot where she had seen the jungle man. He was not there. However, one thing was there that shook her to the bot-

tom of her soul: a footprint in soft ground. Jongor's footprint! She had not been mistaken. Jongor had been here!
From this spot, he must have seen her.

But instead of coming to her, he had turned and had
gone in the other direction!

She did not try to understand the meaning of this. For
her, at this moment, understanding was impossible. The
emotional load within her was so heavy that she could
not even think. Suddenly her emotions burst the dam she
was attempting to impose on them and was washed out
in hysterical sobbing and tears. Sitting down at the base
of a tree, she cried her heart out, saying over and over
again: "I don't understand it! I just don't! Why would he
do a thing like that?"

She was sobbing so heavily she did not hear Umber
approach or come around the tree until she looked up and
saw him. With him was the whole band of Murtos, including Great Orbo. As she stared at him, Umber
pounced like a great cat and grabbed her.

"See!" Umber shouted at Great Orbo. "At night, she
ran away like I told you. Now I have caught her, for
you!" Umber was bursting with pride.

"Uh," Orbo grunted. "Probably you helped her escape
in the first place!"

"No!" Umber denied. "I chased her in the night but
she hid from me. Now I have found her again."

Ann Hunter said nothing. In her the gloom was too
deep for words. Now that Jongor had ignored her, she
did not care what happened to her.

It was Calazao who made an important discovery. The
giant pointed to the soft ground. "Look! Footprints!" he
grunted. Instantly he identified the prints in the soft soil.
"Jongor! He has been here!"

The Murtos had been exulting at capturing Ann Hunter. The sight of the footprints in the soft soil, and the
giant's quick identification of them, silenced them. Instantly hands took a better grip on a spear, tightened
over the handle of a club, reached to make certain the
knife was at the belt. Instantly keen eyes began to search
the surrounding trees, the underbrush near and far, the

stretch of swamp dimly visible from this spot, searching for the jungle man.

Jongor they feared. Jongor they hated. Jongor they wanted to kill.

"He was coming for this female," Umber said. "He saw me coming—and ran away!"

"Hunh!" Great Orbo grunted. "Maybe he ran from all of us, or from me, but from you! Hunh!"

"He didn't run from any of you!" Ann Hunter said. "He'll come back! You wait and see!"

"If he is going to come back, why did he run now?" Umber demanded. "Why didn't he stay and face me?"

"I don't know," Ann answered, miserably. "But it wasn't because he was afraid of you! There's something wrong with him. He's sick. Or hurt—"

"Hurt?" Great Orbo demanded. To him, to all the Murtos, the prospect that Jongor was hurt and could not fight was good news indeed. "We will catch him!"

It was Calazao who pointed out a possible defect in this line of reasoning. "The tracks do not say he is hurt," the giant said. "If he was limping, the tracks would show it. If he had been wounded, there would be blood!"

"Um!" Great Orbo said, thoughtfully. "You are right, Calazao! Well, we have his female. If we take her with us, he is certain to follow. We will set another ambush for him. This time we will catch him!"

The thought of capturing or killing Jongor excited Orbo very much. As though this job had already been accomplished by thinking about it, the Murto leader strutted back and forth, his tail jumping and curling and his chest thrust out in anticipation of coming triumph.

From the depths of misery, Ann Hunter listened to this talk. Deep in her heart, she was certain that this would be one ambush that would not work—if she could do anything to prevent it! But if the Murtos set an ambush, she tried to comfort herself with the thought that Jongor would not follow her and would not try to save her. At the thought that he had deserted her, the misery engulfed her again as she dissolved once more into tears.

Forcing Ann to go with them, and very much alert for

the possible appearance of Jongor, the band of Murtos moved away into the jungle.

Ann Hunter did not know what would happen to her. Nor did she care!

As Jongor moved away, he suddenly realized that the gray ghost was back again in his mind. It seemed to him that it was struggling hard to attract his attention. Perhaps it wanted to talk to him!

At this moment, it did not seem strange to him that an image in his own mind should want to talk to him. In his world at this time this was the way things worked. Ghosts came into your mind and talked to you. Perhaps other people called these ghosts *thoughts*, perhaps still others called them *memory*, perhaps, still others even had different names for them. The names people had for them did not matter to him. What did matter was that this phantom was back in his mind and was tugging, somehow, at his heart strings.

Did he know this woman in his mind, this strange female that seemed to be trying to attract his attention? "My mother is the only woman I have ever known," he told himself.

Instantly the phantom in his mind seemed to try to grab him and shake him. Hard, as if she was determined to attract his attention.

At the same instant, like heat lightning seen far away in a dark night, he had the impression that he knew her. "Ann?" the single word came unbidden to his lips.

At this word, the ghost in his mind smiled at him and nodded strongly.

"Who are you?" he whispered.

"I'm Ann," she answered. He saw her lips move, he felt her words as thoughts within his mind.

"Who—who—who—?" The single word formed a stutter of sound. "Who are you?"

"Jongor! Don't you know me?" the image questioned.

He shook his head. "I seem to know you—but I'm not sure."

As he was speaking, denying that he knew her, he was aware that the image was slipping away from him. Per-

haps his words of denial had shoved it from his mind.
Perhaps some other force had acted in such a way as to
wash the image from his consciousness. Whatever the
reason, it slipped away.

When it was gone, he was suddenly incredibly lonely
in his own land. Coming from out of the depths of his
subconscious mind, emotions for which he had no name
swept over him, such longing as he had never known,
such homesickness as he had not known existed.

He told himself that he did not know this woman, that
she meant nothing to him, that he had never seen her before in all his life. As these thoughts came into his mind,
he knew them to be lies. He had seen her somewhere!
But where? Perhaps she would know! If he went back to
her and asked her when and where he had known her—

Instantly, he turned back along his trail, returning to
the spot where he had seen the woman in the tree. She
could tell him about herself. Perhaps she could even tell
him something about him!

The sounds of Murtos up ahead told him to be wary.
Keeping out of sight, he approached the monkey-men.
Great Orbo was there, and Umber, and that giant! None
of them were friends of his!

They had the female with them, as a prisoner. He
watched them take her away. When the band was out of
sight, he considered what he would do. Shrugging, he
told himself that what they did with this young woman
did not matter to him, that he did not know her, that he
had never seen her before. As he reached this conclusion,
tumultuous protest shrieked at him from his subconscious mind.

Ignoring the protest, he resumed his course toward the
great cave where he had spent his childhood. Instantly
the protest from his subconscious mind grew louder. Be-
wildered, he listened to this tumult. It was as if something that he could not see or feel or hear, some strange
entity that was just below the level of consciousness knew
more about what he should do than he did!

"Follow her!" a voice shouted at him from below. "Follow her—and find yourself!"

"But it is none of my business—" he told himself.

"It is your business!" the voice shouted from below.

"Those Murtos are dangerous," he hedged. "And that giant with his battle axe—"

"Damn the giant and his battle axe!" Now the voice from below sounded like that of his father, as he remembered it from childhood. "You are Jongor! You do not desert your friends!"

"Is she a friend of mine?" he asked.

"Except for your mother, the best friend you ever had!" the voice shouted at him.

"Well—" Jongor began.

"Follow her!" the voice said.

"Do I know her?"

"You most certainly do!"

"I can't remember her."

"Follow her and find out who she is," the voice said.

"Who are you?" Jongor asked. To this question he was given no answer. Indeed, the question itself seemed to drive the voice out of his mind. Like the ghost of the woman, the voice slipped out of his mind, fading away behind an invisible barrier that he could no longer penetrate.

Now, for the first time, he began to get the impression that something was wrong with him. "Am I sick?" he wondered. Living close to nature, sickness was a word for which he had little understanding.

One thing was now certain in his mind. He would follow the woman. He told himself this was only because of curiosity but he sensed that under the curiosity was another nameless driving force.

Chapter VII

Alliance Between Enemies

The Murtos had not gone far with Ann Hunter when they heard an excited clamor ahead of them. In this land there were always many sounds, the chatter of monkeys in the tree tops, the screams of birds, the hoarse bellows of bull alligators from the swamps. Any creature that hoped to stay alive in Lost Land had to be able to identify any sound instantly.

Great Orbo only listened for a split second to the chatter coming from ahead. "It is my people," he said. "It is the rest of my band."

"What are they so excited about?" Umber asked.

"How would I know? Perhaps they have seen a large snake, perhaps one of the swamp monsters has come upon dry land. Nobody but a fool would ask such a question," the leader replied. "We will go and see."

They went forward cautiously. As soon as they were in sight of the band, the reason for their excitement was immediately obvious.

"Look! They have found two men like Jongor!" Umber called out.

"Two more of those murdering humans!" Great Orbo said. "Where did they catch them?"

"I'm not sure they have caught them," Umber answered. "These strangers have those strange weapons called *guns!*"

71

"Where would they get guns?"

"Perhaps they brought them with them."

"Where did they come from?"

"Nobody but a—" Umber started to say, then hastily changed his mind. Looking at his chief's bulk and knowing Orbo's nasty temper, Umber decided it would not be wise to echo Orbo and say that nobody but a fool would ask such a question. "I do not know, Great One. There seems to be some far-away land where these white-faced monsters live, but I do not know where this land is located. Nor do I wish to know."

"Go forward and signal to our people that we are here and that two of them are to come to us," Orbo said.

"They will listen better if you go forward and order them to come to you," Umber said quickly.

"I will stay here," Orbo said. "You will go." Suggestively, Orbo fingered his club. Neither Murto mentioned that the guns of the white strangers were the real reasons for staying well out of sight while somebody else went forward.

Grumbling, Umber obeyed his leader. When the other group saw him, they gestured for him to come near. The two humans waved at him. Umber in turn waved at the group.

"Two of you, come here; Great Orbo orders," he shouted.

Two Murtos left the other group and came to Umber. He took them to Great Orbo.

"These two humans came to us," the Murtos explained. "They made signs of friendship."

"And you let them approach you?" Orbo demanded.

"They were already close enough to talk when we first saw them. They said they had heard in a far country of Great Orbo and wished to meet him."

"Well!" Orbo said, softening.

"They said they wish to learn from Great Orbo," the messengers said.

"Oh!" Orbo said. This information pleased him.

"They also say their guns are at the service of Great Orbo," the messengers continued.

"Then let them approach," Orbo decided. "But all of

you stay near me, with spears and clubs ready, to destroy them if they attempt to use their guns on us!"

When he mentioned guns, Orbo spoke with awe and respect. Other humans had brought guns into this land and the Murtos had learned about them by bitter experience. Some of the weapons of the long-gone civilization of the ancient Murians still existed but the degenerate Murtos understood very little about them and knew even less about using them. Over the centuries, as the old-time technicians died, as eventually the capable repairmen began to fail to train their sons in the ancient skills, the Murtos had forgotten how to repair the equipment that their forefathers had built in other days. Clubs and spears and knives were their limit in the way of weapons.

Urged, the two white men came close. They looked with surprise at the giant, Calazao, then they bowed humbly to Orbo, thus flattering his ego. They made signs of friendship and signs of submission. The Murto language they could not speak. Then they saw Ann Hunter. Instantly they backed a step away.

"Where did you get this woman?" the bigger of the two asked.

"They captured me!" Ann Hunter said, speaking for herself. "They have no right to take me! Take me away from them!" As she was speaking, in English, she was trying to free herself from the Murtos who were holding her.

This effort failed. She simply was not strong enough to pull herself loose from the powerful Murtos.

"Shoot them!" she shouted at the two men. "Shoot him Orbo,—I mean!"

She did not know these two men but at this moment, anybody who spoke English was automatically her friend. They would help her, she knew! They belonged to her own race!

The two men stared at her.

"What do you make of it, Jake?" the shorter one asked.

"Damned if I know, Emil," the taller one answered. "These are the missing links we came here to find but the last thing I expected to find living among them was a white woman!" He looked closely at Ann. "Are you really a white woman? Or are you another freak like that so-called white man who called himself Jongor?"

In all that he said Ann Hunter heard only the word: *Jongor!* "Have you seen him? Where is he? Did—did something happen to him?"

She spoke in English. Not understanding this strange language, the Murtos stared at her. The two white men understood the words perfectly but they also stared at her.

When they did not answer, Ann continued to speak, blurting out words that perhaps had little meaning but which adequately expressed the emotional turmoil within her.

"Where is he? I want to find him. If he's hurt, I'm the one to help him."

"Speak so all can understand," Umber said, in the Murto tongue. "Great Orbo does not like this silly talk."

"How do you know what Great Orbo likes and does not like?" Ann snapped at him, shifting quickly to the Murto tongue. "If I told him about you turning me loose so you could have a better chance to rub noses with me—"

"What?" Orbo shouted, lifting his club.

"It is a lie, Great One," Umber screamed, backing away.

"Do you understand this monkey talk?" the taller white man asked.

"Yes."

"How'd you learn it? How do you happen to be here? What's your name?"

"My name is Ann Hunter. What's yours?"

"Why, I—" Taken aback at the sudden question, the tall man hesitated. "I'm Jake Gnomer." He nodded to his companion. "This is Emil Rouse. We're scientists who were sent here to study these monkey-men."

"You don't look like scientists to me," Ann answered. "You look like thugs. Where did you see Jongor?"

"Well, we may look a little rough," Gnomer answered. "But our porters ran off with all our gear—"

"Where did you see Jongor?" the young woman interrupted.

"Well—" Gnomer did not like these questions nor did he like the way they were being asked. Under other circumstances he would have slapped such a questioner to the ground. He did not slap Ann Hunter because he saw where she could be useful to him. Very useful!

"I don't know what this jungle man means to you, Miss Hunter, but he came into our camp one night—"

"Was he hurt? Was he wounded?" Ann interrupted.

"Not that I could see," Gnomer answered. "He promised to guide us to the lost city of the Murtos, then—" The burly man shrugged. "He simply refused to keep his word. Instead, he ran away from us." He shrugged again, more elaborately. "We thought something was wrong in his head. Ain't that right, Emil?" he asked his companion.

"It sure is, Jake," Rouse heartily agreed.

"I'm sorry, Miss Hunter," Gnomer continued.

Sick in his head! At these words, Ann Hunter felt her spirits sag again.

"If you will translate for us—" Gnomer began.

"I'll try," Ann said, wanly. Great Orbo was already speaking. She listened to what the Murto leader was saying.

"He wants to know what you are doing here in his land," Ann translated.

"In the great world outside, we heard of the might of the Murtos," Gnomer said, Ann translating. "We have come to live with them, to learn from them, and, if we can, to help them."

"Will you help us do something right now?" Orbo questioned.

"If it is in our power!"

"Something is following us," Orbo said, the young woman translating as he spoke. "We want you to take your guns—" The Murto leader pointed to the weapons. "—and shoot him!"

"I suppose he knows he is asking us to commit murder?" Gnomer said.

"In this land there is no such thing as murder," Ann anwered. "There is only death."

For only a second, Gnomer hesitated, not because he was concerned about the ethics of murder but because he had another question on his mind.

"Who is it that he wants shot?" Gnomer asked, Ann translating.

"Jongor!" Great Orbo answered, as soon as he understood the question.

In utter dismay, Ann Hunter realized what she had done. In this moment, if she had had a gun, she could have killed Gnomer and Rouse. And Great Orbo!

Great Orbo was greatly excited at the prospect of having two guns to help him get rid of the feared and hated enemy.

"Shoot him and you shall have your choice of anything the Murtos own!" he told the two white men. "Gold, diamonds—anything!"

"What did he say?" Gnomer asked Ann.

"He said for you to go to hell!" she answered.

For a moment, Gnomer backed a step away from her. Then he took a step toward her, his hand lifted as if to strike her. Two Murtos were holding her. She made no attempt to pull away from Gnomer. The Murtos in their turn made no effort to protect her.

"What did he say?" Gnomer repeated, pointing to Great Orbo.

"He said he would have you killed as soon as let you shoot Jongor," Ann answered.

"You're lying!" Again Gnomer's arm went up as if to strike.

"If I am, what are you going to do about it?"

This time Gnomer fully intended to strike. She made no effort to escape.

It was Orbo who intervened. The leader stepped in front of Gnomer. Waving his club, Great Orbo shouted at the burly man in the Murto tongue.

Gnomer moved back again. This time he did not ask Ann to translate what the Murto leader had said. Instead, bowing and grinning from ear to ear, the burly man made placatory signs to the leader of the Murtos.

Great Orbo understood those signs to mean agreement to his idea that an ambush be set for Jongor and that the two men would shoot the man from the jungle.

"We will lay the ambush in a place I know," Orbo said. He considered himself to be an expert in the matter of laying ambushes. This one he laid with special care. First, the entire group of Murtos went forward through a narrow gap between two hills, making certain they left tracks in many places, and making doubly certain that their female captive left tracks too, for Jongor to follow.

After this was done, Great Orbo posted Gnomer and Rouse with their rifles on the hillside overlooking the gap. He sent Umber and a group of Murtos armed with spears to the hill on the other side of the gap. Ann Hunter and several of his band he kept with him.

Great Orbo could hardly conceal his excitement. Anyone following the trail of the Murtos would have to come through the gap. Anyone who came through the gap would meet the far-striking death from the deadly rifles.

Orbo was very pleased to have men with rifles fighting on his side. He considered that the Great Unknown God had sent them to him to enable him to destroy his enemy. He was voluble with promises of what he would do for Gnomer and Rouse as soon as Jongor was dead.

"Gold, diamonds I will give you," Orbo promised the two men. "All you can carry away. However, do not kill this Jongor too quickly. Let me finish him off with *this!*" He lifted his heavy club.

"What did he say?" Gnomer demanded of Ann Hunter.

"He said for you to go to hell!" she replied.

"Stop it!" Gnomer shouted at her. "I'm getting tired of this kind of talk from you!"

"Shhhh!" Rouse urged his partner. "I caught a glimpse of Jongor at the far side of the gap!"

"Where?" Gnomer demanded.

"At the far end of the gap," Rouse answered. "It was just a glimpse. I don't see him now."

Across the gap, Umber could be seen making signals that he had seen something.

The group crouched in the shrubbery of the hillside. Gnomer and Rouse found a rocky ledge that they used as a rest for their rifles. Orbo crouched out of sight. The two Murtos who held Ann forced her to the ground. From this position she could not see what was happening in the gap. All she could really see was Gnomer on his knees behind the rocky ledge, his eyes along the sight of the gun and his finger on the trigger. Just beyond him Rouse was also kneeling with his rifle ready.

Far off in the jungle a bull alligator bellowed. Or was it a crocodile? Ann knew there was a difference between alligators and crocodiles but at this moment, the difference had no meaning for her. Wings buzzed near her and a brightly colored hummingbird dropped down to sip at an orchid's nectar. She watched the two men. In the sky above a buzzard circled slowly on motionless wings as if it sensed that soon food would be ready for it on the ground below. Orbo was squatting so near her that she could hear the rumblings in his stomach. Her attention was concentrated wholly on the men with the rifles.

"Remember, we're shooting downhill," Gnomer tersely commented to his companion. "Aim low."

"Think I'm a fool!" Rouse grumbled.

"There he is!" Gnomer whispered.

Both men instantly lined up their rifles.

As they did this, Ann Hunter screamed.

Instantly, the two Murtos who were holding her shoved her face into the dirt. She didn't care about that. The purpose of her scream had been to warn Jongor. The important thing was that she had accomplished her purpose, that she had warned him.

A split second after she had screamed the two rifles thundered in unison!

She heard Gnomer swear, then the guns roared again.

She tried to scream again but the two Murtos had shoved her face so deep into the ground that she could hardly breathe.

Upon entering the gap between the two hills, Jongor was well aware that this was the kind of place where the Murtos loved to wait in ambush. It did not concern him greatly. His feeling was that if Murtos waited here now, let them be the ones to look out! Their spears and clubs he could dodge but they could not so easily dodge his arrows!

He wanted to know about the woman the Murtos had captured, who she was, where she had come from, and what she was doing here in his world. He also wanted to know why she should so much resemble the phantom that moved like a gray ghost in his mind!

Most of all, he wanted to know why she should pull so heavily at his heart strings.

"What is this woman to me?" he asked himself.

Then, from the hillside, he heard her scream!

Without knowing how he knew it, he realized that her scream was meant as a warning to him. He did not look for Murto spears coming toward him. He assumed their existence—and threw himself on the ground.

It was not Murto spears that went over him. It was something that hissed like angry hornets through the air. He recognized the sound. Bullets!

Because the bullets were moving faster than sound, he heard their howl through the air above him before the roar of the guns got to him.

Murtos with rifles! The thought dazed him! A second later he knew that more than Murtos were on the hillside! Men with guns were there!

One guess told him the probable identity of those men. Gnomer and Rouse! They had found the missing links they were seeking and had made friends with them!

He wasn't facing spears and clubs, he was facing rifles!

He rolled to the side. Bullets thudded into the dirt where he had first dropped. Getting to his feet, he ran. Bent double, he ran like a halfback in a broken field. As if he was dodging tacklers, he veered to the left, then to the right, never going straight away from the rifles. Bullets whistled through the air around him.

Seconds after the first shots had been fired, he was back in the trees on the far side of the gap.

In his mind were confused thoughts. He had tried to make friends with the two men and they had held him captive at gunpoint. He had followed this woman—and the two men had tried to kill him.

These two thoughts condensed into one thought which became a conviction—people were dangerous!

Chapter VIII

In the Murto City

As the rifle shots roared, Great Orbo rushed at Ann Hunter. The two Murtos who were holding her face against the ground got hastily away. They did not like the fact that Orbo had his club high in the air nor did they like the looks of his open mouth.

Sitting up, gasping for breath, Ann Hunter did not like the look of the club or of the open mouth either. Orbo had fangs at least three inches long.

Her first thought was that he intended to use the club to knock her brains out.

At that moment, gasping for breath, hearing the rifles thundering as they hurled slugs at the jungle man, she did not care if he did kill her. If Jongor was dead—and the rifles were still thundering—death now would only release her from other, more unpleasant, and slower forms of death to come later.

When she saw the club over her head, she made no effort to resist.

This saved her life.

If she had tried to dodge, if she had tried to get to her feet and run, if she had lifted a hand, if she had even used her voice to protest, Orbo would have struck with the club. This was a deadly weapon. She would never have survived one blow from it.

But she didn't move, she didn't try to run, she did not lift a hand to ward off the blow. All she did was look up. She faced a fanged mouth roaring at her, she faced two eyes red with rage, she faced an uplifted club—and did not flinch.

In a circle, Orbo danced around her. Now that the rifles were thundering, he could roar too. Roar he did, in great bellowing shouts of pure rage. Ann Hunter gave no sign that she even heard him.

Suddenly the rifles were silent. Gnomer and Rouse, rising, ran along the slope of the hill.

Orbo followed them.

Ann got to her feet. Kego seized her and threw her back to the ground. The second Murto sat on her stomach. No matter how much she writhed and twisted, she could not dislodge the monkey-man. Meanwhile, dread was rising in her as she waited for more rifle shots. These did not come but their absence proved nothing. Perhaps Jongor had been killed by the earlier bullets! In that case, there would be no more shots. All there would be would be Orbo and his club beating a wounded or possibly a dying man to death.

She listened for the sound of blows. None came. Eventually she heard men talking as they returned. Gnomer and Rouse were arguing with each other.

"I tell you I winged him!" Rouse was insisting.

"Then why didn't we find blood on the ground?" Gnomer asked.

"I don't know. But I hit him with my last shot! You can bet on that!"

"Hell, you couldn't hit a sitting elephant!" Gnomer answered, his voice hot with anger.

"I didn't see you doing so much better!" Rouse answered, equally angry.

"I would have hit him with the first shot if this damned broad hadn't screamed and warned him!" Gnomer said. "Where is she? I've half a notion to—"

Great Orbo arrived at the same time. It was Orbo who roughly ordered the Murto to get off Ann's stomach. Orbo screamed at her to get up but she was too weak to stand. Kego and his fellow Murto guard yanked her to her feet. Ignoring her, shouting at Umber to bring his group from the far hillside, Orbo stalked ahead.

"What—what happened to Jongor?" she asked Gnomer, when she had the strength to speak.

"How the hell do I know what happened to him!" Gnomer answered.

"You—you didn't kill him?"

"Hell, after you screamed, he jumped around so much we didn't even come close to him," the burly man answered. "And it's all your fault!"

Hope came up again in her heart. Jongor was still alive. In her mind was the certain thought that he would come eventually and rescue her.

She asked the two Murto guards about Alan. Kego snarled at her to shut up. The other guard said nothing. "We haven't seen him" Kego said finally.

At the first opportunity, she asked Umber about her brother. Umber was the Murto Alan had fought in the darkness at the base of the tree where she had tried to hide.

"Him?" Umber had to think hard to remember the person she meant. "I don't know where he is. I guess I killed him." Umber shrugged the question aside as being of no importance. "And I'll get that other one, that Jongor, too! You wait and see." He leered at the young woman. "Why don't you forget him? Why don't you choose me instead? I'm stronger than this Jongor, and more handsome! I'm braver—"

"You'll run if you even think Jongor is within miles of you!" Ann answered.

"Hah! I will not!" His bushy tail waving in the air, Umber strutted back and forth beside her. He flexed his arm muscles to show how strong he was.

"If you get close to me I'll call Great Orbo!"

"Huh? Him?" Umber sneered. As he was speaking he was looking in the direction of his chief. Great Orbo was at the front of the group and was out of hearing distance. "Some day I will bash in his skull. Then I will be chief!" At this thought, he began to strut again. "Then you will be mine."

"I'll die first," Ann Hunter answered.

When night came, the Murtos stopped to camp in the hills. At dusk they busied themselves gathering and eating a fruit that looked much like bananas. Gnomer and Rouse also ate this fruit. Kego and hiss fellow guard allowed Ann enough freedom to find and eat fruit.

The two men, Gnomer and Rouse, gathered wood for a fire. All night long the Murtos were uneasy, becoming alert at each sound. Ann Hunter was also aware of every sound. Any noise might be her brother, or Jongor, coming for her.

When the sun came up, she was still a captive of the Murtos.

For days the march continued across Lost Land. Gnomer and Rouse talked often to the Murtos, with Ann doing the translating. To refuse to translate would only get her beaten, she knew. Gnomer was very curious about the science of the ancient Murians, the ancestors of the monkey-men. Did any of the old instruments still exist? Were there libraries of old books which explained the instruments? Ann could find no word in the Murto language for *books*. Apparently the very concept had faded from the degenerating minds of the monkey-men.

Ann had little interest in this talk. Her eyes were continuously on the back trail. Seeing her doing this, and guessing who she was looking for, Gnomer and Rouse, their rifles always ready, also watched the back trail.

"I don't want this jungle man spoiling everything now!" Gnomer said. "If you warn him again, I'm going to shoot you first."

"Orbo will club you to death if you do," she told him.

"As long as I have a gun, Orbo and his club take a back seat," Gnomer said. There was so much bitterness in his voice that she backed away from him as much as possible.

They reached the top of a rise from which the city of the Murtos was visible.

The old, old town sat in a valley between hills. Back of it was a tall cliff from which the ancient Murians had mined gold. To the left, a swamp came up to the edge of the city. What was now swamp had once been an arm of the sea. Ruins of an ancient harbor were dimly visible.

Here ships had once docked with supplies for the colonists of this city. Here the same ships had been loaded with gold for the Motherland of Mu.

Walls surrounded the old city. Inside were many buildings, most of which had fallen into ruin. Broad avenues were still visible. From them rose two and sometimes three story buildings made of stone. Here in these buildings was housed what was left of the ancient scientific equipment of the Murians. From one of these buildings the tornado-like vortex called *the shaking death* could be launched, if the ancient equipment still worked. There was another structure which had once housed a very unique form of airship. Whether it was still there or not, Ann did not know. In attempting to rescue her the last time, Jongor had almost wrecked the building.

Would he rescue her again? Her eyes went along the trail they had followed. Nothing moved there.

The terrible stench of the city rose to meet them. She remembered this smell, which was a mixture of garbage and sewage, from her previous trip to this place. Just as people who have taken a steamer to China will say that you can smell China two hundred miles off the coast, so the old city of the Murtos could be smelled from miles away.

Orbo was greatly excited at the sight of his city. "Home!" he said, in his language. "The greatest place on Earth! Home!" He gestured downward. "It even smells good!"

"Has that Murto gone crazy?" Gnomer asked Ann, in English.

"No crazier than usual," she answered. "He grew up in a stink and to him a stink is a good smell."

Gnomer seemed hardly to hear her answer. His attention was concentrated on the city. Interest was strong in his eyes.

Rouse was not so strongly impressed. "It don't look like much, Jake," he said. "Are you sure this is the place?"

"As I remember the aerial maps which we lost, this is it, all right. If the city is here, maybe the things we are looking for are here too!" Eagerness grew stronger in the voice of the burly man.

"What aerial maps are you talking about?" Ann Hunter asked.

"High-flying jet planes are mapping the whole world," Gnomer explained. "Some lucky pilot got a shot of this place when there were no clouds over it. We saw those maps."

"What was in them that brought you across the deserts and into this land?" Ann asked.

Rouse glanced at Gnomer. Both men fell silent.

"Forget I ever said anything," Gnomer spoke.

"What the hell difference does it make if she does remember what you said?" Rouse questioned. "She'll never be able to tell anybody about it. We could even tell her what the old legends say is hidden here—"

"Shut up, Emil!" Gnomer said.

Rouse muttered something and fell silent quickly. Gnomer began to ask Ann questions about the city. Listlessly, she answered. He did not ask about the gold she had seen there, or the jewels. Instead his questions seemed to be devoted exclusively to what she had seen of the old machines of the ancient Murians.

"I really don't know," she told him. "I'm not an engineer or a scientist. What little I saw, I didn't understand. What is supposed to be there?"

"Old scientific equipment that the world has lost," the burly man told her.

A babble of sound from the Murtos pulled his attention away from her. For this, Ann was grateful. Then, when she saw the objects that were causing the Murtos to call out in sudden fear, she was not grateful.

They were standing on a long ridge. Below them was the ruined Murto city. On their left, the long ridge sloped down to the swamps.

The Murtos were pointing to their right along the ridge. Looking in that direction, Ann Hunter saw moving objects in the distance.

At first, she could not recognize what was moving there. Her attention was pulled away from them by the alarmed yells of the Murtos. Kego and his companion let go of her arms—and fled down the hill toward the old city. A single glance told her that all of the Murtos were fleeing in the same direction, including Great Orbo and Umber.

"What the devil is wrong with them?" Gnomer asked.

"They saw something that scared the wadding out of them," Rouse said. He was staring along the ridge. "There!" His hand lifted to point. "What the hell—"

"Dinos!" Ann Hunter shouted, recognizing what was moving there in the distance.

Coming along the ridge, now out of sight as they swerved around an outcropping of rock, now in sight again as they found the going good, were three dinosaurs. These were not the vegetation-eating specimens that Gnomer and Rouse had encountered earlier. These were the meat-eaters, the terrible thunder dragons of antiquity, still surviving here in Lost Land in very limited numbers.

These were the creatures that could eat a deer for breakfast and be hungry again before lunch. These were the monsters that could tackle the great cave bear and the saber-toothed tiger of long ago, that could meet the elephant and the wooly mammoth on even terms. These were the biggest and most deadly killers the planet had ever known!

These were the creatures that the Murtos had seen coming along the ridge and which had sent the monkey-men into wild flight to reach the protection of the walls of their city. And these were the monsters that had made the Murtos forget completely that they had men with guns to protect them!

When faced with three thunder lizards, the Murtos lost all confidence in guns!

"What are we going to do, Jake?" Rouse demanded.

"Climb trees!"

"There ain't any trees!"

"Then we'll climb that rock there!" Gnomer pointed to a stone pinnacle about fifty yards on their left. This stone outcropping was perhaps thirty feet high. On top of it, they would probably be safe. The dinosaurs could not climb where a human could.

"Come on, Emil!" Gnomer said, backing away.

Rouse hurried to move away. Gnomer turned, then stopped and looked back for Ann Hunter. The young woman had not moved. Instead she was staring at the on-rushing dinosaurs.

Something there had caught her attention. Clinging to the neck just behind the fanged mouth, riding like a cowboy bent low in the saddle, was a human!

Instantly, she recognized this human.

"Jongor!" she screamed. He had not followed her! Instead, he had gone into the jungle and had found three thunder lizards and had brought them here to lay in wait for the band of Murtos!

"Oh! Him!" Gnomer said. "He is controlling those monsters! And I know how to stop them!"

Lifting his rifle to his shoulder, Gnomer's eyes went along the sights. His target was the rider on the lead dinosaur.

"Stop it!" Like an enraged tigress, Ann Hunter threw herself at the man. Grabbing the gun barrel, she jerked it down. The gun thundered but the bullet buried itself into the ground.

"Damn it!" Gnomer struck at her with his fist, and missed. She went in under his arms and grabbed him around the middle with both arms. Clawing, kicking at his legs, she clung to him. He could not lift the rifle to shoot again and she was so close to him he could not hit her with his fist.

In her mind was the single thought that if she could hold on to this man for even a few minutes, Jongor would arrive with the dinosaurs. She did not know what would happen then. Perhaps he would snatch her from the arms of this man and would ride away with her. Perhaps the dinosaurs would trample both of them!

"Damn you, let go of me!" Gnomer was trying to force her away from him. He brought the rifle barrel down over the top of her head. The jarring thud from the gun made her think her brain had exploded. In spite of this, she held on. Getting both arms around his neck, she locked her fingers behind his head. Then she clasped both legs around his middle and locked them behind his back.

Gnomer struck at her. He could get no strength into the blows.

The thunder of running dinosaurs grew louder.

It was Rouse who grabbed her hair and yanked on it with all his strength. Agony shot through her scalp but she still held on. Striking with his fist, Rouse struck her savagely on the side of the head. Stars exploded in front of her eyes. She felt her grip loosen on Gnomer. Then she was on the ground and trying to sit up.

Near her, she heard a rifle roar. Then Rouse was shouting. "Got him! Got him, Jake, with the first shot!"

Looking to her right, she saw the dinosaurs. Vaguely she was aware that the first one was now without a rider.

"By God, you did get him!" Gnomer acknowledged.

"And you said I couldn't hit an elephant!" Rouse shouted.

The dinosaurs were coming closer. Now the thundering of mighty feet was very clear. Also audible was the sounds they made, a high, thin, shrill noise that was vaguely similar to the trumpeting of an elephant.

On the ground, Ann Hunter stared at the charging monsters. She knew only too well what would happen to anybody caught beneath those pounding feet.

She was too choked, too hurt physically and emotionally, to try to get to her feet. Hit first by a bullet and knocked from the lead dinosaur, Jongor had to have been trampled to death by the two monsters following the first one.

The stampede of a herd of cattle was nothing in comparison to the charge of three dinosaurs. Jongor might have survived the wound from Rouse's bullet, but nobody could possibly survive the impact of those thundering feet.

"Hey, Jake! Those damned monsters are still coming!" Rouse shouted. "I thought you said that this Jongor could control them!"

"If you got Jongor, they should have stopped," Gnomer said.

"Well, I got him—and they didn't stop!" Rouse said. He looked back at the pinnacle of rock. "Hadn't we better get back there?"

"We sure as hell had!" Gnomer answered. He grabbed Ann Hunter by the arm. "Come on, witch! Let's get out of here!" When she refused to budge from the ground, he began screaming at her, asking if she wanted to get killed.

"Yes," she answered.

"Are you out of your mind?"

"Perhaps. But in a choice between you, the Murtos, and death, I prefer to take death." Her voice was a gasping whisper that was almost inarticulate.

"Well, you're not going to die yet," Gnomer answered. "Here, Emil, take my rifle." He tossed the gun to Rouse. "I've got to carry this broad!"

Ann Hunter found herself being lifted and thrown over the shoulder of Jake Gnomer. With Rouse running ahead, they moved toward the safety of the pinnacle of rock.

Ann Hunter did not see Rouse stop running. Thrown over Gnomer's shoulder, she could not see anything. The first intimation she had that everything was not right came when Gnomer bumped into Rouse so heavily that the burly man stumbled and fell, dropping Ann at the same time.

"You damned fool!" Gnomer said. "Haven't you got enough sense to get out of my way—"

"L—l—look!" Rouse whispered.

Gnomer looked and was suddenly silent. Ann Hunter looked—and did not believe her own eyes.

Jongor stood in front of them. He blocked their passage to the rock pinnacle. The great bow bent to its farthest extent, the arrow nocked on the string was centered on Gnomer's heart.

"But—but—but I shot you!" Rouse whispered.

"You shot a bundle of leaves and some reeds made into a figure that would look like a man from the distance," Jongor answered. He looked at Gnomer and suddenly shifted the arrow to center on Rouse.

"Drop the guns!" Jongor said.

"Y—yes," Emil Rouse whispered. A gun—Gnomer's rifle—went to the ground.

"Jongor!" Ann whispered.

Involuntarily, the eyes of the jungle man went to the woman on the ground. In the split second when Jongor's full attention was not on him, Rouse centered his rifle on her.

"If you shoot me, Jongor, I'll shoot her!" Rouse whispered.

Jongor's attention came back to Emil Rouse. He saw the rifle, he saw Rouse's finger on the trigger, he saw the determined expression on Rouse's face. He did not move.

In the background along the ridge great feet thundered closer each minute.

"Drop the bow or I'll kill her," Rouse said. "I mean it!"

The great bow stave creaked as Jongor slowly released the tension on the string. Triumph lit Rouse's face. "Now drop the whole thing!" he said.

The bow and the arrow tumbled to the ground. Gnomer grabbed his rifle.

The thunder of the charge of the approaching dinosaurs was growing louder.

"Keep her covered, Emil!" Gnomer said. His own rifle centered on Jongor. He jerked his head backward along the ridge. "Turn 'em aside!" he said. "Or both of you will die! And don't try to tell me you can't control them because I know that you can do it!"

Jongor's eyes went to Ann Hunter. With Rouse's rifle covering her, she was getting to her feet. A strange expression was on her face, a mixture of fear, or longing, and of the sight of heaven suddenly opening.

"Jongor!" she whispered. "You—you did come to rescue me!"

He did not answer.

"I'm warning you—" Gnomer said.

"All right," Jongor said. He did not look at the crystal worn in the gold bracelet on his left wrist. To do so would be to run the risk of getting shot because he had moved his arm. Instead of moving, he visualized the crystal clearly in his mind, then concentrated his attention on it.

To those watching him very intently, he seemed to be doing nothing. If his mind was reaching through the crystal to the three dinosaurs pounding closer with each fleeting second—and it was—perhaps the only indication of this fact lay in a slight deepening of the gray eyes of the jungle man.

The thunder of feet grew louder.

"Stop them, I said!" Gnomer's voice had a sudden shrill note in it.

To all outward appearances, Jongor did not even hear the man.

"I'll kill you—" There was no question that Gnomer meant exactly what he said.

"Rouse will shoot her!" Gnomer continued.

Jongor lifted one hand. "Listen!" he said.

The thunder of hoofs was dying. The wailing sounds of the great beasts were changing. Jongor gestured toward his left, the direction of the old Murto city, then waved his hand in that direction.

Down there great hoofs were thundering. Fifty yards away, downhill, in the direction of the old Murto city, three great animals trumpeted as they swept by. Changing direction, they moved directly toward the old city. The screams of Murtos began to come back. Down there, Great Orbo and his band were running for their lives.

Jake Gnomer wiped sweat from his face. Behind him, Rouse did the same. "God, Jake, if those things had got us— Whew!"

"Get his hands tied behind his back. We'll take him with us down into the old city," Gnomer directed. "Tie the woman's hands too—" The voice of the burly man went silent as he watched what was happening.

Ann Hunter had moved to stand facing Jongor. Her eyes searching his face, she stood looking up at him.

"Jongor!" she whispered.

In return, his eyes searched her face.

"Who—who are you?" he whispered.

"You don't know me!" she gasped.

He passed a hand across his forehead. "Sometimes it seems that I do. Sometimes I see in my mind a ghost that looks like you. But—" A frown came over his face and he shook his head. "Who are you? I followed you because I wanted to find out who you are."

"Then—then you didn't come to rescue me?"

"I—I didn't know you needed to be rescued," he answered.

Rouse started to speak but Gnomer motioned him to silence. Below in the distance the screams of the Murtos trying to run from the dinosaurs were dying into silence. "Keep still and listen," Gnomer said to Rouse. "Both of these people know things I want to know, this Jongor in particular—"

"But he's wrong in the head!" Rouse protested.

"Yes, I know. But I think the doctor has just arrived."

"Doctor?" Rouse protested. "I don't see any doctor. Do you mean this broad? She's not a doctor, is she?"

"Not so far as I know. But so far as I have seen, if there's something wrong with a man, it'll be a woman who helps cure it, if she didn't cause it in the first place. I don't think this happened here."

"What did happen?"

"I don't know. Keep your mouth shut and listen!" The muzzle of Gnomer's rifle never ceased covering Jongor.

"I'm Ann Hunter," the young woman was saying. Her face was smudged. Lines of fatigue were deep in it. As she spoke to the jungle man, the lines were deepening in her face.

"Ann?" Jongor whispered the word. "It seems as if I heard this word, once, long ago and far away. But—" Strain was on his face. He shook his head.

"Can't you remember me?"

Again he shook his head.

"Can't you remember Alan, my brother?"

"Alan?" Again the questioning look came over Jongor's face, to be followed by the inevitable head shake. "For an instant, I thought I remembered him, but now it's all gone."

"Did something happen to you?" Ann persisted.

"To me?" Jongor's right hand went to the back of his head. "I—I don't remember." Very gently, he rubbed the back of his head.

"Does something hurt there?" Ann questioned.

"Well—sort of."

"Turn around and lower your head and let me look."

Without question, he obeyed her. Very gently, her fingers probed through the hair. He winced and would have drawn away if she had permitted.

"Jongor! There's a bad bruise here! Were you hit on the back of the head with something?"

"Hit?" Standing up, he thought about the question, only to shake his head again.

"If anybody hit me, I don't remember it," he said.

Ann would have asked other questions but Gnomer interrupted.

"There's one thing I want to know," Gnomer said, looking at Jongor. "How do you control those dinosaurs?"

Jongor thought about the question. His eyes said he was thinking. But he answered the same way as before. "I can do it," he said. "I know I can do it."

"How do you do it?"

"I do it in my mind. Inside me, I tell the dinosaurs what to do and they obey me."

"Do you expect us to believe that?" Rouse demanded. Jongor shrugged.

"I don't think he knows how he does it," Ann said, defensively. "I don't think he knows anything any more." She was very close to tears.

Gnomer nodded. "That's my estimate of the situation." He looked at Jongor. "You had a spear. Where is it?"

"I lost it somewhere," the jungle man said. A sad expression on his face, he was looking at Ann Hunter.

Gnomer turned to Rouse. "You tie 'em up while I keep 'em covered," he said.

"Tie 'em with what?" Rouse asked. "We ain't got any rope, Jake. And no wire."

"Use the string off of that bow," Gnomer said. "Get his knife out of that pocket in the skin he wears around his middle. Get anything else that looks dangerous. Take that quiver full of arrows off his back—"

Rouse obeyed. With one end of the bowstring he tied Ann's hands behind her back, with the other end he tied Jongor's hands in the same way.

"This leaves them tied together," he said to Gnomer.

"That's all right," the burly man answered. "If they're tied together, one won't run away without the other."

"What are we going to do with 'em?" Rouse asked.

"Trade them to the Murtos, if nothing else," Gnomer said. "Move along, you two. And if those dinosaurs come too close, remember I'll shoot both of you."

Neither answered him. Neither seemed to have heard him speak. Obediently, they moved down the slope toward the ruins of the Murto city.

Chapter IX

Captives

The dinosaurs were not seen as they approached. However crunching sounds were to be heard in a tree-filled ravine to their right. Rouse listened to these sounds with great apprehension.

"It sounds like a bunch of dogs gnawing on bones down there!" he said.

"Probably Murto bones being gnawed down there," Gnomer said. He looked at Ann and Jongor ahead of him. "Those dinosaurs had better stay down there in that gulch!"

Jongor glanced around. "They'll stay down there until they get hungry again. This won't happen until tomorrow."

"W—will they come looking for us tomorrow?" Rouse asked.

"They'll be looking for something to eat but not us," Jongor answered.

They went over the wall at a low spot and were in the Murto city. The stink here was stronger. Trees were growing now in what had once been broad, stone-paved streets. The city was silent. The Murtos had seen the *big-mouthed death*—their words for the thunder lizards —and did not wish to come into the open as long as these creatures were in the vicinity of their city. Finally, in response to Gnomer's shouts, a single Murto appeared. It was Orbo. The Murto leader looked down the street in both directions and nervously fingered his club. He seemed not to notice Jongor and Ann and was hardly aware of Gnomer and Rouse. He had something else on his mind.

"The big-mouthed killers, where are they?" he asked.

Ann had to translate his question in English, then had to translate Gnomer's answer back into the Murto tongue.

"Back there in a ravine eating Murtos," she told Orbo.

The Murto leader shivered at this news. He started back into the stone building from which he had emerged but was stopped by Gnomer's voice.

"Tell him we want a place to stay. Tell him we also want a place where you and your boy-friend can be locked up. Tell him we want a Murto with a club to stand guard over you and Jongor." Gnomer's voice grew harsh. "Tell him anything else and you will live to regret it."

"Right now I'm regretting even being alive," Ann answered. However, she translated Gnomer's instructions as best she could. Still very nervous about the big-mouthed death, Orbo had difficulty in understanding what was wanted. When he got the idea, he summoned Kego and gave him instructions. Kego took them to the old mine workings in the cliff behind the city. Here were a number of small cells opening from a large corridor. Kego ordered them into one such cell, then closed and barred the iron-grill door. He took up his position in the corridor outside.

Gnomer and Rouse moved across the corridor and set up camp in another cell, one which had no door.

Water was brought to them, and fruit. Kego shoved the water container under the door of the cell and shoved the fruit with it.

"We can't eat when our hands are tied behind our back," Ann pointed out.

"Lap it like dogs," the sullen Murto told them. Nor could they get Kego to change his mind. Shouts to Gnomer and Rouse brought no response. Eventually they lapped the water. The fruit they ate by bending over and biting it.

Both were utterly exhausted. They slept back to back, hands touching. Awakening now and then, Ann was aware that Jongor's finger's were working with the bow-string. The string that held the force of the great bow would not break but it might slip. Under Jongor's fingers, slip it did, eventually. Ann felt the bow-string loosen around her wrists. Not until she tried to move her arms did she realize how much pain was in her shoulders. Rolling over, she worked the bow-string loose from around Jongor's wrists. In the darkness, she heard him grunt with relief.

Outside the grilled door of the cell was night, black and complete. In the cell across the corridor Gnomer and Rouse had built a fire but it had long since died to a bed of coals. With his bottom on the floor of the corridor, his back against the cell door, and his club held in his lap, Kego snored.

They lay very close to each other, whispering.

"I still don't know who you are," Jongor said.

"Oh, my poor dear!" She put her back against the wall and pulled his head into her lap. "Now tell me about yourself, all you can remember."

"But you seem already to know about me."

"I do."

"Then why should I say it again."

"Because telling me again may help you to remember." She was stroking his forehead as she was speaking, hoping to help him find himself. To please her, he began to talk, telling her again about his parents and how he had got his name.

"Are you my mother?" he asked suddenly.

"No," she told him. Her voice was firm but very kind.

"You are like her." His voice was that of a tired and confused child. "I want to call you *mummy*."

"It is best if you call me Ann," she told him. "Tell me about life here in Lost Land."

He answered with a full description of all he had seen and done here. "I like the dinos best of all," he said.

"They are my best friends." Again his voice was that of a child.

Ann Hunter had no knowledge of psychology but in trying to help this man, she was obeying instincts deep within her, instincts that said a hurt, lost child needed love and attention, someone to make it feel secure. In this situation, she also knew that she needed someone to make her feel secure too! Perhaps if she gave security, she might find it for herself. She knew without question that her only hope of escape, perhaps her only hope of life itself—if there was any hope of this—lay in this big man who had lost his memory and who persisted in trying to live in the fantasy fairyland of a child.

"Tell me more about your life here," she told him again and again.

With his head lying in her lap, he was as obedient as any child could have been. But he just couldn't remember. A segment of his life was missing.

"Remember, outside Lost Land, when the Black fellows were attacking, who you met there," she said.

He twisted in her lap at this. For a moment, she thought he was going to remember. Then he shook his head again.

Bird calls outside the old mine shaft announced the coming of dawn. Kego turned his snore into a snort. Awakening, the Murto guard went to the entrance of the tunnel.

"We will put the bowstsring back around our wrists and put our hands behind our back, so that no one will know we are no longer tied together," Jongor said.

"What good will that do?" Ann protested.

"Even if I cannot remember you, I still have strength in my muscles," Jongor said. "Perhaps, if they think we are still tied together and helpless, they may not guard us so closely."

"Do you think there is any chance at all that we can escape?" Ann asked.

He shrugged. "Who knows? But my mother always said that the only way anything got done was by trying."

"You must have had a wonderful mother!"

"I did." His voice grew distant. "And somehow you remind me of her."

"I know." Her voice slipped away into silence. Across the corridor, Gnomer and Rouse began to stir the bed of coals. Kego returned and took up his position outside the door. Eventually Gnomer and Rouse left the cavern. Gnomer stopped long enough to say they were going out to look at what could be seen in the ruined city.

"I'll want you later, to do translating for me," he said to Ann.

She watched the two men tramp through the corridor. Her mind moved to the fate of her brother. She did not doubt that Alan was dead somewhere in Lost Land. In her mind was the thought that she would soon join him. The Murtos would kill Jongor, and her too, as soon as Gnomer permitted, which would be as soon as he no longer had a use for them. Even if Jongor should manage to escape, he would spend the rest of his life wandering through Lost Land wondering who he really was and what had really happened to him.

RrrrrrrrRRRRRRRrrrrrrrrRtttttttttRTRTRT!

The sound that brought both Jongor and Ann to their feet was a scream similar to the warm-up howl of a jet engine of enormous horsepower. Muted by distance, the roar seemed to come from beneath them and from deep inside the workings of the ancient mine. The tumult of sound moved through the corridor outside. It was so strong that the solid stone floor under their feet picked up the vibrations.

The sound also brought Kego to his feet. Holding his club ready, he backed against the crossed bars of the iron door. Kego seemed to think that something would soon be coming along the corridor. He would have run if he had dared.

Reaching through the iron grillwork, Jongor caught the Murto by the throat and pulled his head and shoulders against the bars.

"Uch!" the Murto grunted. This sound had started out to be a yell for help but fingers as strong as steel bands were clamped around his throat. These fingers turned the yell into a grunt. Jerking and turning, Kego tried to pull free. The fingers held him. Getting one leg up behind him, he shoved backward against the bars of the door. The fingers still held him. Lifting his club he tried to strike backward at the hands and at the wrists that were reaching through the bars. This failed. He dropped his club. Reaching upward, he caught the wrists of the hands that were holding him. All Murtos were very strong. Kego was no exception. As Kego pulled downward on his wrists, Jongor felt sweat begin to pop out on his skin. He got one knee against the iron grill. Using this as leverage, he began to pull backward. At the same time, he tightened his grip on Kego's throat.

"Shove the bar out of its sockets!" he whispered to Ann.

She moved quickly to obey him. Reaching through the grill, she worked with the heavy wooden bar, pushing and shoving at it. Kego's back against the bar was making her task difficult. She pushed harder. The bar slipped out of its sockets and fell to the floor of the corridor. An inch at a time, Jongor began to shove the door open, doing this without loosening his grip on Kego's throat. When the door was open enough to permit it, Ann ran outside.

"Get his club," Jongor said.

She picked it up and would have smashed the Murto on the head with it but Jongor stopped her. "Don't knock him out! I want to talk to him. He's getting weaker!"

Jongor's memory might have been gone but he still had his strength. When he released the Murto and Kego sagged downward to the floor, he was out the door so quickly that he was standing over Kego before the latter could even move. "Give me the club," he said. Silently, Ann handed it to him. He held it ready as Kego gulped for air. When the Murto was sitting up, Jongor showed him the club. Kego tried to shy away from it.

"I want the truth," Jongor said. "What was that sound?"

"Voice of—Great Unknown God," Kego whispered. He spoke with difficulty, possibly because he was still struggling for breath, possibly because he did not want to say the words because of superstitious fear that it was dangerous to speak aloud the name of any god.

"Where is this god?" Jongor demanded.

"Down there—" Kego gestured toward the depths of the mine.

"I never see him but I hear about him. God of old miners. He dug gold for them. Or so I have been told. Not been down there myself."

"Who's down there now?" Jongor asked.

"Not know. No Murto!" Vigorously, Kego shook his head. He looked longingly at his club.

Jongor had not forgotten how to speak the Murto tongue. "It sounds to me more like a devil down there. Tell me more about this devil, or this god, that lives down below."

"Not know, not know, not know." It was hard to tell whether Kego was more afraid of the club in Jongor's hands or of the wailing sound that had come from down below. It was easy to tell he was in abject terror. "All I know is that when Great Unknown God calls, a sacrifice must be made ready."

"Hanh?" The grunted sound was a question in any language. "What means this sacrifice?"

Kego did not want to answer his question. He squirmed and twisted and tried to get to his feet. Jongor tapped him with his own club, not really hard, just hard enough to make his head ring like a deep-toned bell, and he answered the question.

"Someone sent down into pit to serve god!"

Jongor did not understand this. Ann supplied another possible meaning to the Murto words. "I think he means a living human—a living Murto is tossed down an ancient mine shaft to appease what they think is an angry god," she said. A shudder passed over her face. "These Murtos are utter savages!"

"I know," Jongor said. He opened the door of the cell and spoke to Kego. "In there."

Kego crawled through the door. Instructed by Jongor, he lay flat on his face. Ann tied his hands with Jongor's bow-string. Closing the door, they slipped the big wooden bar back into place, then turned toward the outside.

Dark figures moved at the end of the corridor, blotting out the daylight there.

"I guess we won't go outside," Jongor said, recognizing these figures. "I guess we will go that way!" He pointed inward along the corridor.

"Hold it, hold it, hold it!" a voice rang out. When they did not stop a rifle thundered and a bullet howled past their heads to go screaming down the corridor, knocking sparks from the stone walls as it bounced from them.

Jongor would have kept running. He seemed hardly to know the risk of stopping a bullet. Ann caught his arm. "Please! To try to run here is to die!"

This stopped the jungle man. Behind them, feet were pounding. Gnomer and Rouse came up. With them were Great Orbo and Umber with eight or ten Murtos. Orbo had recovered his lost courage. Gnomer looked as if he had just achieved the aim of his whole life.

"Trying to get away, huh?" Gnomer demanded. "How'd you get out of that cell?"

"Where Kego?" Orbo spoke. Gnomer did not understand him but Umber did. On the run, Umber went back to the cell, to look inside. His scream announced that Kego had been found. Minutes later, Kego had been released from the cell and was coming toward them, rubbing his head and yelling how he had almost been killed. Seeing his club in Jongor's hands, he demanded it be returned to him. Jongor, aware of the rifles, lifted it. Thinking Jongor was threatening him with it, Kego backed hastily away. Shrugging, Jongor dropped the club on the floor. Only then did Kego dare to pick it up.

Watching the Murtos, Ann Hunter saw there was an air of great excitement among them. They were both exhilarated and scared. Orbo did not scream at Kego for almost letting the prisoners escape. Missing a chance to scream at somebody who had made a mistake was not like the leader of the Murtos. The fear on their broad faces was not like the fear they had exhibited when they had fled from the dinosaurs but was of a different kind. They were afraid but they were also very eager.

She could not understand the Murtos. Nor did she have time to try to understand them.

RrrrrrRTRTRTrrrrrrrrrrrrRTRTRT——

Like the scream of a gigantic siren, the roar of what Kego had claimed was the voice of the Great Unknown God came rolling up from the depths below.

Instantly every Murto was flat on the floor and was rubbing his nose in the filth accumulated there for uncounted centuries. Only Jongor, Gnomer and Rouse, and Ann Hunter remained standing.

"These superstitious fools—" Ann heard Gnomer mutter.

"Jake, there are thousands of them and only two of us," Rouse protested. Rouse was almost as scared as the Murtos. "Jake, I'd rather get away from this place."

"And leave behind us one of the greatest discoveries ever made on Earth?" Gnomer demanded. "Don't be a damned fool!"

"I'd rather be a live damned fool than a dead smart man!" Rouse answered. "What *is* that scream?"

"They think it's the voice of a god," Gnomer answered. "You and I know better." A shadow crossed his face. "What we don't know is who is goosing the god to make him roar like this!"

"Maybe he's goosing himself!" Rouse said.

"You utter fool! That would mean the god is real, that he is intelligent, that he can decide for himself!"

Rouse gestured at the Murtos flat on the floor. "These monkey-men think he is real," he said.

Fear crossed Gnomer's face. "That can't be true," he said. "It just can't!"

The distant roar screamed itself into silence. The Murtos rose. Orbo pointed down the corridor. "This way," he said. Fear and eagerness were again mixed on his face.

"You go ahead of us," Gnomer said to Jongor and Ann. "If you try to escape, I'll shoot to kill."

Ann looked back toward the entrance. Back there Murtos were swarming into the corridor.

"The whole tribe is following us," she said to Jongor. "What does it mean?"

"I do not know," the jungle man answered. "I have

never been down here before. I do not know what the Murtos do when they come here."

Ann spoke to Orbo, trying to question him. Orbo's eyes measured her.

"We go to make sacrifice to the god that lives below," the Murto leader answered.

"What does that mean?" Ann continued.

"Soon enough you find out," Umber answered, for his chief.

Chapter X

The Horror Below

When daylight ended in the corridor, the stored torches were brought out. The Murtos each took one and lighted it.

"Get light for you too," Orbo said, to Ann. "For others."

Jongor took a torch without hesitation, Gnomer and Rouse with reluctance. Obviously the two men were afraid the flaming torch might interfere with their handling of their rifles. Other Murtos crowding into the corridor also took torches. Holding the lights aloft, these Murtos raced on ahead, to disappear into side tunnels. When Orbo moved forward, the Murtos holding Jongor by the hands shoved him ahead too. Ann was also forced forward by Kego. Gnomer and Rouse were now directly behind Orbo. Umber and other Murtos brought up the rear.

Orbo went down a flight of steps. Worn, these steps were, by feet that had passed up and down them in ages past. More flights of steps were ahead. Orbo went down. And down. To the left a long tunnel slanted outward. Gnomer hesitated long enough to identify the tunnel.

"This was an ore chute! Long ago ore went down this chute straight into the holds of ships docked outside in what are now swamps." He thrust his torch into the sloping tunnel and rubbed its bottom with his fingers. Dust inches deep was there. Gnomer rubbed the dust away and stared at the floor of the tunnel. "Just the gold that rubbed off the ore left that chute lined with yellow," Gnomer said, half to himself.

"How much gold did they mine here?" Rouse asked.

"How they mined it is more important than how much!" Gnomer said.

The descent seemed to end as Orbo moved forward again. Ahead was darkness. And silence. And a feeling of enormous dread. Walls that had been vaguely illumined by the torches seemed to move back and away. Ahead was a metal balustrade. Moving very carefully Orbo thrust his torch into a wall socket. Umber and the other Murtos found other wall sockets.

Ann moved toward the balustrade. Kego pulled her away from it. Below was darkness and a feeling of great depth.

"I think we're on the edge of the old mine pit," she heard Gnomer say.

Now, below them, other torches were appearing. At the sight of them, Ann knew that the Murtos who had turned off to a side tunnel had gone farther down. One by one they were slipping torches into wall sockets. Illumined by the torches, the whole vast area was vaguely illumined.

And how vast it was! An enormous circular hole had been dug there. Ann looked over the edge of the platform where she was standing and backed hastily into Kego, who was also trying to back away.

In the middle of the vast excavation a hulked monster squatted.

"That's the digger!" Gnomer said, staring.

Rouse gestured upward. "How'd they get the ore from down there up to the chute?" he asked.

"How the hell would I know?" Gnomer answered. "They dug the ore electronically!"

"How'd they get it up to the chute?" Rouse persisted.

"Sometimes you're so damned stupid, you're smart!" Gnomer said. "Come on! We're going down there!"

Jerking torches from the wall, Gnomer and Rouse

turned away. Orbo shouted at them to stop but they did not understand the Murto words. Before Orbo could speak again, coming from above, a scream stopped his speech.

Coming downward, a heavy object struck the edge of the balustrade in front of them, bounced outward from it, screamed again—and fell downward.

"That's a Murto!" Ann gasped.

"Yes!" Kego whispered. "He jumped from above."

"Jumped?"

"Yes. He offered himself as the first sacrifice." Kego's teeth were chattering as he spoke. His arms were shaking so badly that he hardly gripped Ann's arm.

Thump!

The sound that came from below was solid. And heavy. And final!

Down there somewhere a Murto had struck a stone floor. Death had certainly been instantaneous.

A moment of silence followed the thump. Then came sound, enough of it to fill the whole vast cavern, sound made up wholly of spontaneous outpouring of moans from the thousands of Murtos gathered at many balconies around the huge mine pit.

At the sound, Ann Hunter found that she was beginning to shiver. In the sound somehow, was a feeling of pain greater than the mind could bear, a feeling of ancient hurt that cut deep into the emotional world. The Murtos gathered here had seen death. They had seen one of their members seek death—and find it in the solid thump down below. In the moan, also, was something of a longing for past glories. The race that had dug this mine pit, that had lifted ore upward to be dumped into a chute which fed it into the holds of waiting vessels, the ancient Murians, the ancestors of the Murtos gathered here, had been great, once. No doubt about it! Somewhere on a vanished island empire, they had dug deep into the secrets of nature. Perhaps they had even probed the stars! They had dreamed great dreams.

When the home islands had gone under the Pacific Ocean, the colonists here had been left alone. With only their own resources to fall back upon, they had taken the slow trail that leads downward to oblivion, that leads eventually to the death of a people.

In the moan that went up from the assembled Murtos was the lament that they had turned backward. They did not understand what had happened to them. All they knew was that somewhere they had stumbled and had fallen—and that their lot was now to inherit death.

Whether death came to them of their own free choice —as it had to the Murto who had hurled himself downward as a willing sacrifice, did not matter. It would come eventually to them as individuals. They moaned because of this. It would also come to them as a people. They also moaned because of this.

Hearing what was in this vast moaning wail of lamentation, for one mad second, Ann Hunter almost felt sympathy for the Murtos. Almost, but not quite! In her mind was one clear thought—that she and Jongor would eventually become unwilling sacrifices to the Great Unknown God of the mining pit. Perhaps they would be given a chance to leap from this balcony. If they refused to leap, they would be thrown off it.

In the moan of the Murtos was also the fear of death. And something else! An effort to avoid it by sending somebody else in their place! The scapegoat was here! With their sacrifices of others, the Murtos were trying to buy more life for themselves.

On the floor of the cavern, torches moved. Gnomer and Rouse were down there.

Instantly silence filled the cavern. Ann Hunter moved closer to Jongor. Kego permitted this movement. She saw that the two Murtos holding the arms of the jungle man were watching what was happening down below.

Fear was suddenly in the cavern, a cold wind of it. For two foreigners to approach the Great Unknown God in the center of the cavern was something that had never happened before. The Murtos waited. Perhaps the great god would blast them for this sacrilege!

"Hold your torch higher," Gnomer said, as he and his

companion approached the hulked machine in the center of the cavern. Rouse obeyed. Gnomer stopped to study the machine.

To the right a long snout poked out. The nozzle of this snout was pointed downward to the floor of the pit.

"They sent a blast of some kind of energy out of that snout and concentrated it on the raw rock," Gnomer said. "They used some kind of an electron flow to separate the metal from the rock right at the point of contact!" Excitement was strong in his voice.

"What's that there?" Rouse asked, pointing to a bulky box at the rear of the machine. A hopper led into the box. "That's where they dumped the ore from the machine," Gnomer said.

"How'd they get it up there to that chute?" Rouse asked, pointing upward.

"Another stupid question. They hooked it to a derrick that lifted it up to the chute!" Gnomer said. "Hold your torch high. I want to go up into the cab where the controls of this digger are located."

"Are you sure it's a machine?" Rouse questioned.

"What else could it be?" Gnomer answered. He moved forward. A flight of steps led upward to the control room. As he moved up the steps he was aware that silence gripped the vast cavern. He gestured upward at the Murtos. "They're too scared to breathe!"

"Me and them both!" Rouse said. "I keep remembering that howling sound that came out of this place."

"It came from right here," Gnomer said. He climbed into the cab. In the front of the cab were many control levers. He began to study them.

"If it came from right here, what caused it?" Rouse persisted.

"It was a siren of some kind. Equipment like this is always fitted with some kind of a device to give warning when it is in operation."

Rouse thought about this answer. It had flaws in it. "If it was a siren, who turned it on?"

"I don't know," Gnomer snapped. "Now shut up and let me study this thing."

But Rouse was not to be quieted. He looked down at

the floor of the cab. Dust there was inches thick. "Look at the marks in that dust!" he said, almost stuttering.

"So, there are some marks in the dust. So what?"

"But who made them?"

"Some Murtos slipped down here and started this machine by accident," Gnomer said.

"No Murto would come down here!" Rouse answered. "And if he did, he wouldn't know what to do to start this machine—if it is a machine."

"Maybe he started it by accident," Gnomer said. He looked around the cavern. Under the light of the flaring torches nothing was moving. Near the wall a blotch on the floor revealed the body of the Murto who had fallen or—who had been thrown—from above. Near it were patches of skin stretched over broken bones, the relics of previous sacrifices here in this dark place.

"I don't see anything," Gnomer said. He turned his attention back to the controls. "This one turns something on. If there is enough juice—and these old engineers must have had something very like atomic power, which will last forever—" He pushed the control forward.

RrrrrrrrrRTrrrrRTRTRTrrrrrr. . . . .

The scream of a gigantic siren filled the vast cavern. Electric fire leaped from the nozzle outside. Concentrated downward on the floor, the intense electron flow seemed literally to blast the rock out of existence. Metal in a molten form was sucked upward by a powerful vortex.

Gnomer hastily pulled back on the control lever. The scream of the siren went into silence. Echoes came back from every wall of the deep pit.

Then another sound came. Alarmed, Gnomer and Rouse both looked up. A vast wail that was the product of many throats came from the ledges up above.

"It's only the Murtos howling!" Gnomer said.

"*Only* the Murtos howling!" Rouse answered. "Listen!"

Screams were coming from the ledges up above. Up there, Murtos were leaping downward to death. The leaps ended in heavy thumps on the stone floor of the cavern.

"Damned fools!" Gnomer said. "They probably thought their god was calling to them!"

"You don't suppose they threw Jongor and that woman off the ledge, do you?" Rouse demanded.

"If not now, then later," Gnomer replied. He turned his attention back to the controls of the machine.

"J—Jake, I don't like it here," Rouse whispered.

"Run if you want, you won't run far," Gnomer said. "You damned fool! Don't you realize that this machine is actually a laser beam better than anything known in the world today? And the Murians had it thousands of years ago!"

"Hey, look!" Rouse shouted, pointing to the rear of the machine.

The bulky box-like container at the rear of the machine was slowly rising in the air. Gnomer stared at it. "What's lifting it?" he whispered.

"Maybe there's a derrick up overhead," Rouse ventured.

"You fool! We would have seen it."

The container was now well above them and was rising slowly but steadily. The Murtos had seen it. The sight had driven their screams of lamentation into silence.

Gnomer was suddenly shouting. "Emil, do you know what we're seeing? Emil, it's the biggest thing ever discovered! Emil, that's worth more than all the gold the Murtos ever mined out of this mountain! Emil—" Gnomer choked on his own eagerness to talk.

"What the hell is it?" Rouse demanded.

"*Anti-gravity!*" Gnomer's shout rang through the whole cavern. "Don't you know what that is?"

"I've heard of it but I've never seen it."

"You're seeing it now! When this digger operated, it threw the separated metal into that container. The container then carried the metal up to the chute, dumped it, and came back down here for more gold. All done automatically! I tell you, Emil, this will make us both so rich we won't be able to count our money!" Gnomer was wildly excited. In his mind were visions of all that unlimited wealth meant to him, power, property, women—but mostly power. With the secret of anti-gravity under his control, he saw himself heading a corporation that ruled transportation on Earth—and possibly to the stars! With anti-gravity, railroads would not be needed, vast freighters would no longer pound their way through stubborn seas, truck and bus lines would go out of existence. If a small unit could be perfected, the individual automobile would either go out of existence or would be so radically modified that it would no longer be recognizable.

Anti-gravity would change the future of the human race! This much was certain.

"I've got it right here in my hands!" Gnomer shouted.

Rouse was watching the bulky container. It had swung off to the right. "It's wobbling," he said.

"It hasn't been used in a long time," Gnomer said. "It's still rising, ain't it?"

"Yeah. But—"

"But what?"

"I was just thinking—" Rouse pointed again to the floor of the control cab. "Whoever made those tracks there, we ain't seen him yet."

"So what? Some Murto—"

"What if he's in that container?"

"He can't be!"

"We didn't look inside it."

"It's automatic!"

"Maybe it's not automatic. Maybe there are controls inside it. Maybe whoever made those tracks in the dust is in there, running it!"

"You get above that car and see who's in it. Go back up the way we came down. Leave your torch here." Gnomer was giving orders quickly and decisively. "I'm not going to find something this big and then let some damned monkey-man—"

"What if it's not a Murto in the container?"

"It's got to be!"

"It ain't got to be no such thing!"

"Get up above that container! Whatever is in it, shoot it!"

"What if there's not anything in it?"

"If it's not automatic, then somebody is in it operating it," Gnomer said. "Shoot whoever is operating it!"

"But, Jake—"

"Git, damn it, before I shoot you myself!" Gnomer said, lifting his rifle.

Sticking his torch behind a holder on the outside of the control cab, Emil Rouse fled. There was enough light from the thousands of torches for him to see clearly. Above him, the container moved erratically. He entered the same tunnel that he and Gnomer had used in coming down. This would take him to Jongor and to Ann Hunter, to Orbo and to Umber. Perhaps one of these could tell him why the container was moving! He doubted if he had the courage to face Jake Gnomer again without an answer. What was moving that thing? Emil Rouse could not think of any solution that pleased him. If engines were in it that defied gravity who was running the engines? Or what?

It was the *what* that really scared Emil Rouse. In his present frame of mind he was quite willing to believe a god lived in this vast pit. Or a devil!

On the balcony, Ann Hunter clutched Jongor's arm and tried to attract his attention. Kego was too disturbed to try to stop her, and the two Murtos guarding Jongor were too shaken by the death screams that ended in heavy thumps to notice what was happening.

Jongor was also interested. "Did they jump?" he asked her. "Did their friends throw them off? Why would they do that?"

His voice was still that of a child. A curious child, perhaps a frightened child. But more curious than frightened. A wide-eyed child who wanted to see what was going on. A child who kept pushing closer to the balustrade around the projecting balcony. A child who had no hesitancy about elbowing Murtos to one side.

"Jongor!" Desperation was in Ann Hunter's voice. "Remember who you are!"

"I know who I am," the jungle man answered. "I'm Jongor." The child was pleased to answer this question.

"That's not what I mean!"

"I want to see what's down below," Jongor said. He shoved hard on a mountain of fur-covered meat. Great Orbo himself was too disturbed by what was happening down below to resent being shoved. He reached the edge of the protective railing. Ann had no choice except to go with him. The metal of the railing was almost corroded away. She noticed this. The child Jongor may have noticed it but he did not think it was worth thinking about.

"What's that moving down there?" the child asked. Jongor pointed downward.

Looking down into the pit, Ann could see where a container of some kind had detached itself from the monster in the middle of the excavation. The Murtos were watching it too, with intent interest. Was this a messenger sent up to them from the god below? They began to moan again, a low, whimpering, wailing sound.

The dark container began to circle the inside of the pit. Staring at it, Ann had the impression either it, or somebody inside it, was searching for something. Perhaps for a way out! Jongor watched it.

"There's a gap in your memory," Ann said to him. She had read that children could be given instructions in their sleep. "I want you to remember what happened during that gap."

"A gap?" He seemed to answer without real understanding. "What is a *gap*?" His eyes did not leave the dark container. It was now directly below them. "There's somebody in that!" he said, suddenly.

"What difference does that make?" Ann asked. She was too desperate for tears. "It's Gnomer. Or Rouse."

"Gnomer is down below. I can still see him. Rouse ran to a hole in the pit some time ago." The child was excited but it was still observing closely.

From a lower balcony, a spear was thrown at the dark container. Metal striking metal rang like a bell. The container kept rising. The Murtos moaned louder.

Somewhere behind her, Ann could hear a man panting heavily, like a dog that had run a hard race. Rouse, shoving Murtos out of the way with his rifle, came poking forward. "I want you," he said to Ann. "Jake wants to know what that dark thing is?"

"I don't know."

"Ask him." Rouse poked Great Orbo with the muzzle of the gun.

Ann spoke to the Murto leader, then interpreted for Rouse's benefit. "He says he doesn't know either. He thinks it is a messenger from the Great Unknown God— or from the great unknown devil. He doesn't know which."

Another spear leaped out. It struck metal too and fell away to the floor far below. The dark container kept rising. Directly in front of the ledge, and perhaps five feet away, its movement stopped.

On top of it, a protective metal cover was thrust aside. Inside the container, something rose, to stand there staring at the group.

"A—a man!" Orbo gasped.

The man in the container opened his mouth to scream two words at the top of his voice.

"*Jongor! Sis!*" the man shouted. "Jump into this atom-powered go-buggy and we'll get the hell away from here!"

Ann Hunter gasped. The rider in the dark container was her brother Alan, whom she had thought dead. Somehow he had made his way to the city of the Murtos. Somehow he had found an entrance to the ancient mine pit!

Ann was not concerned how this was accomplished. All that mattered to her was that it had been done!

Beside her she heard the jungle man gasp. "That's Alan. And now I know who I am!"

"Throw her to me, Jongor!" Alan screamed. "I'll catch her."

Near her, she was aware that Rouse was lifting his rifle to his shoulder to shoot the rider in the dark container. Beyond Rouse, Orbo was drawing back to throw his club. In the background, Umber was lifting a spear.

But to Ann Hunter, the most important thing was that Jongor had suddenly gasped—and had recovered his memory!

Chapter XI

Battle to Death

Just as Jongor did not know what had caused the loss of his memory, so he did not know what had caused it to return. All he knew was that when Alan Hunter had yelled at him from the interior of the container, memory had come flooding back. When he had recognized Alan, he also remembered Ann—and everything that had happened between them in Lost Land. It was as if the blow from the thrown club had broken an electric circuit in his brain; so the sound of Alan yelling his name had restored that circuit.

The restoration of that circuit instantaneously gave him back his lost memory. It also gave him back something else that he had lost almost without realizing it was gone—his sense of values. Now that he knew who Ann and Alan Hunter were, he had a reason to fight! He struck out, quickly, at the rifle in Rouse's hands.

Knocked from Rouse's grasp, the gun flew up and out. So close did it fall to the container that Alan Hunter grasped at it. Missing the weapon, Alan almost fell himself, the container teetering from his shift of weight.

Jongor paid no attention to Alan Hunter. Alan was capable of taking care of himself in an emergency. He saw the spear in Umber's hands, he saw the club that Orbo was getting ready to throw. Crowding on to the balcony, other Murtos were also lifting spears or clubs.

Umber did not throw his spear. Something hit him on the side of the jaw, a jolting blow that knocked him dizzy. Umber had not seen Jongor's fist coming. All he knew was that something hit him very hard. Before he realized what was happening, the spear was wrenched from his grasp.

Jongor turned to Orbo. Ann Hunter had grabbed Orbo's arm, preventing him from throwing the club. Orbo had jerked one hand free and was striking down at her with a ponderous fist.

Jongor hit Orbo the same way he had hit Umber, with a jolting blow that had every ounce of his strength behind it. Orbo blinked. Striking at Ann Hunter, he knocked her out of his way. Again he grabbed the club. With both hands on this heavy weapon, he struck at the jungle man with it.

Jongor twisted his head, his shoulders, and his body. There was no time to dodge with his whole body. He simply twisted his body out of line and let the club scrape skin from his left side as it went down.

Then he brought the flat side of the spear down on Orbo's head with all of his strength. Orbo batted his eyes a couple of times as the blow hit—then went down.

From the vast mining pit came a scream. "Hit 'em, Jongor!" Alan Hunter shouted in the container. "Give 'em hell, Yale!"

The shout from Alan brought up an emotional surge in John Gordon. A kind of happiness was in that surge of emotion—happiness because he had his full memory back and was his own man again—plus something else. This something else could perhaps be called the *joy of battle*. There is a joy, almost an ecstacy in some people, which comes from using oneself to the fullest extent of capacity in deadly battle. The old Norsemen knew something of this emotion. When they filled themselves with it, and poured themselves into battle, few enemies ever stood against them.

The same kind of joy, the same kind of battle madness, the same kind of lust to fight, was now in the jungle man.

He was his own man again! All of his life he had had to battle for existence! He could do it again.

"Alan! Catch Ann when I hand her to you!" he yelled.

"Will do!" Alan Hunter yelled in reply. Inside the container, he shifted controls. The ancient ore car nudged closer to the balcony.

"Ann! Quickly!" Jongor turned to pick her up. He faced Umber instead. With long, clawed fingers the Murto lieutenant reached for Jongor's eyes.

In this moment, Umber saw himself as at last achieving his long-sought goal of being leader of the Murtos.

The goal became a grunt of pain as Jongor went in under the reaching, clawing fingers and hit Umber squarely in the stomach with his left fist. As Umber grunted, and bent over in response to the blow, Jongor hit him under the jaw with his right, a savage blow that had all of the jungle man's strength back of it.

Umber did not grunt as he went down. He simply fell backwards. As he was sprawled out, he carried two club-waving Murtos with him.

Jongor lifted Ann. "Trust me," he said.

"I do," she answered.

Lifting her, he tried to hand her to Alan. The distance was too great. He had to toss her. She went through the air, limp, like a rag doll. Catching her in both arms, Alan eased her to the floor of the container.

"Sis, you made it!" he whispered.

"How did you get here?" She demanded.

"After Umber knocked me out, I was dazed. The next day—or maybe it was the next after that—a giant came walking through the jungle. He had a battle axe and was muttering to himself what he was going to do to the next Murto he saw—they had failed to pay him the agreed price for helping them ambush Jongor—"

"Calazao?"

"Yes. I followed him here. He's somewhere in the tunnels up above now, trying to catch Murtos one by one. I found my way down to the bottom of this pit. When I tried out that ore-digger, I almost scared myself out of my mind. I was just exploring this container when Gnomer and Rouse came across the bottom of the pit.

Sis, get off of the controls! Your weight is sending this thing down. We've got to get it up again so we can pick up Jongor."

Ann moved hastily. "I'm sorry, Alan. I didn't know—"

"What you don't know in this place will certainly get you killed!" Alan said. The container was dropping downward. Frantically working with the controls that lifted the clumsy ore car, he looked up. Jongor was looking down at him.

From the bottom of the pit below, a rifle was firing. Alan heard a bullet hit the container. Tortured metal screamed, bounced from the car, howled across the vast mine pit.

"That's Gnomer down below," Alan said. He moved the controls, shoving them as far as they could go.

The car continued dropping. It was a slow drop but a steady one. Whether the current had failed or whether Ann's added weight was more than the capacity of the container could hold, Alan did not know. He looked up.

Up there, Jongor was just launching himself from the balustrade. With the spear held ready in one hand, the jungle man dropped down toward the container.

He hit feet first and caught himself with all the ease of a cat. The container teetered and dropped lower. "Hi, Alan. Hi, Ann!" He looked at Alan. Another bullet struck from below, to howl away toward the wall of the pit. Somewhere in the distance a Murto screamed as the bullet accidentally struck him. The struck Murto thought the bullet had come from the Great Unknown God. Thinking this, he jumped. Eventually a solid *thump* came up from the bottom of the pit.

Whang! went another bullet!

"Send us up, Alan," Jongor said. "There are high tunnels. If we can reach one of these, we can escape into Lost Land. There, if needed, I can call the dinos to our aid—"

Alan's face was grim. He was still working with the controls. "It won't lift any farther," he said.

Whap! went a bullet on the ancient ore car.

"Whether we like it or not, we're going down," Alan said. Desperation was in his voice.

"I see," Jongor said. He looked up and ducked as a spear went over his head, then ducked again as a heavy club came whirling from one of the balconies. The memory of being struck on the back of the head by a thrown club brought back the pain in his head. This was gone in a moment.

Alan worked with the controls. The ore container continued settling. Now, just above the level of the floor, it was moving back toward the machine in the center of the cavern. Was there really something similar to a god about this machine? Would it pull its enemies back to it and destroy them as it chose?

Snap went a high-powered bullet as it literally popped through the air.

The container was down almost to the level of the floor of the pit. Gnomer now had targets for his rifle.

"Keep your heads down!" Jongor shouted.

As the car moved slowly toward the machine in the center of the pit, the jungle man looked upward. The balconies and ledges around the pit, which had literally swarmed with Murtos, were now empty.

He knew what this meant. The Murtos were coming down to the floor of the pit. If the Great Unknown God failed to destroy his enemies, they were going to help do the job!

Whang! went another bullet against the metal hull of the container. This one came from the direction of the wall. "Rouse," Jongor said. "He came down to the floor with the Murtos—and found his rifle. Two guns against us now!" He examined his spear.

The container settled down with a clumping sound. Somewhere relays clicked as they sought for additional energy, then relaxed in tired sounds.

"That's all," Alan said, from the controls. "No more juice."

"Can we cross the bottom of the pit?" Ann asked.

Jongor shook his head. "Murtos there," he said.

"Come out of that thing," Gnomer said, from the control cab of the hulking mining machine. "Come out with your hands up!"

Rising, Jongor threw the spear. The weapon struck

Gnomer, he could not tell where. The rifle thundered, the unaimed bullet going wild. Jongor went right behind the spear, up the machine and into the control cab. Alan and Ann Hunter were right behind him.

Gnomer had dropped the rifle. The spear had struck him in his right forearm and had cut so deep a gash into the muscles there.

At the sight of Jongor, Gnomer went out the far side of the cab. Jongor wasted precious moments finding his spear. By the time he had located it, Gnomer was out of sight in the throng crossing the cavern.

"Look!" Ann whispered.

The throng was made up of Murtos. As she pointed, a thrown spear rattled from the side of the cab. A club following the spear thumped heavily on the metal side of the control room.

Jongor gripped his. On the floor of the cab, Alan found the rifle Gnomer had dropped. Picking it up, he fired into the approaching monkey-men. At such close range, he could not miss.

For split seconds, the fire of the rifle stopped the charge of the Murtos, on one side of the digger. But the ancient mining machine had four sides. To stop the Murtos on one side was not enough. They began to come up the other sides of the machine, climbing it in the same way they would have scaled the side of a cliff.

Great Orbo himself was leading them. Orbo had found another club. With Orbo in the lead, the Murtos would not turn back easily.

To their degenerated, superstitious minds, the great machine in the bottom of the mining pit was literally a god. They did not know their ancestors had built this machine and had worked with it in extracting the yellow metal from the huge vein of ore that lay within the high cliff.

Alan emptied Gnomer's rifle, then turned it into a club.

At the openings of the cab, Jongor fought the Murtos. Spears were thrown at him. He dodged them. He did not throw his spear, instead he thrust with it.

Every time Jongor knocked a Murto off the machine,

another monkey-man took his place. The sound in the cavern was a mixture of wild screaming and doleful howling. To the Murtos, Jongor was trespassing on sacred ground. At any moment they expected the Great Unknown God to blast him. They howled in anticipation of this. However, if the god failed to act, they would do the job themselves. The screaming was in anticipation of this.

Looking over the throng of Murtos, Jongor knew it was only a matter of time. Behind him, he could hear Alan shouting. Turning his head, he glanced back at the youth.

"Alan, didn't you say you had turned this digger on by accident?"

"Yes."

"How'd you do it?"

"There are the controls in the front of the cab." Alan left off swinging the rifle long enough to gesture in the direction he meant. Jongor looked. Ann Hunter was there trying to pull a spear from the resting place it had found. The light of battle was in her eyes. She had no intention of being captured by Murtos again.

With a final shove at the monkey-man who was trying to get into the cab, Jongor dropped down to the floor beside her. As he did this, a rifle roared just outside. A heavy bullet whammed off the metal top of the control cab and dropped harmlessly on the floor, its energy spent.

"Who—" Jongor began. "Rouse dropped his rifle. Alan has Gnomer's gun." He dared a quick look over the edge of the cab.

Gnomer and Rouse were very close. Gnomer had a rifle. Probably this was Rouse's gun he was using.

Jongor ducked back down. "One gun," he said to Ann. "We don't have much time."

"I know," Ann Hunter answered. Somehow, in spite of everything, a smile came on her face. "But you do—" The smile faded a little at the question she wanted to ask. "You do remember me, don't you?"

"Of course!"

"That's all I want to know!" Death was howling outside but in spite of this, happiness came back over her face.

A spear flicked through the cab. Jongor looked at Alan and shouted for instructions.

"Push that lever there," Alan shouted in response. His eyes widened when he realized what the jungle man was going to do. Then his voice lifted in a shout of approval.

"Give 'em hell, Jongor!"

Jongor pushed the control lever.

RRRRRRRrrrrrrrrRT . . . . . RTrrrrrrrrRTRTRT!

Like a gigantic siren, the ancient digging machine screamed its warning signal.

From the snout pointing down toward the floor of the cavern lightning leaped.

The ion fire had already dug a trench almost a foot deep around the digger before the ancient miners had left it. Leaping downward from the snout, the ion fire began to pulverize the rock directly under it.

The fire would also pulverize anything else that was under it.

One Murto was caught in this fire. As though his body had been doused with gasoline and then set on fire, instantly the Murto became a flaming torch.

RTRTRT!

Each time the siren blared, the downward-pointing snout moved perhaps a foot along the trench it had made. The siren itself had been built into the digger to give exactly this warning! The whole cab moved each time the siren blared a high note.

Jongor leaped to the door of the cab. Orbo was there. Jongor struck him with the flat side of the spear. The Murto leader fell, tumbling down the side of the digger. Jongor struck at a second Murto, who also went down. Behind him, Ann Hunter started up. He motioned for her to stay back. "This is not for you to see!" She remained at the bottom of the cab. Alan circled it and stood beside Jongor.

The Murtos, trying to cross the trench, were being slaughtered by what they had called the Great Unknown

God. So heavy was the electronic flow into the trench that all the stone at the bottom was glowing.

"There's thousands of amperes of current going into that rock!" Alan Hunter gasped.

Jongor did not know the meaning of the word *ampere*. Nor was he interested at the moment. Hell was loose in front of his eyes and he was busy watching devils at work. The Murtos could not cross the trench. When they tried it, the heavy current flow through the rock found enough difference in potential between their two naked feet to send heavy flows of electricity up their legs. The result was a paralysis of the leg muscles.

A Murto who fell in this trench, and everyone who tried to cross it fell there, turned almost instantly into a mass of exploding flame.

The stench in the cavern was suddenly almost overwhelming.

Wham! went a bullet past Jongor.

Looking down, he saw Gnomer and Rouse.

Seeing he had missed, Gnomer turned away from the machine. Like the Murtos, he made the mistake of trying to cross the charged trench. The current hit him, froze him. He dropped the rifle. The gun barrel became cherry red. However the weapon did not explode. Apparently there were no cartridges left in the gun.

Rouse tried to follow Gnomer. The current caught him too.

In this way, Jake Gnomer and Emil Rouse died, with incredible flows of electric energy surging through their bodies.

"There goes Orbo!" Alan Hunter said, pointing. "He's trying to jump the trench—"

Rt . . . . . Rt . . . . . Rt . . . . . went the siren, in slowing cadence.

"He didn't make it," Alan said.

"I saw," Jongor said. "And there's Umber."

Orbo had failed in his leap. The electric fire had caught him. For a mad instant, as Orbo's tail jerked frantically, it seemed that every hair on his body had turned into a filament of living flame.

As the flame died out, the stench increased.

"Umber didn't make it either," Alan said.

"There are no more Murtos left on our side of the trench," Alan said.

"I know," Jongor said.

Rt . . . . *Rt* . . . . *Rt* . . . . went the siren. *Rrrrrrt!* It died in a final gasp.

Electric fire ceased pouring from the projecting snout.

"Out of juice," Alan said.

"We had better be out of here, fast," Jongor said. In every direction, the Murtos were fleeing. He looked over his shoulder at Ann, then gave her a hand to lift her up. "Everybody get a spear," he said. "Pick up the Murto spears. Better get two each."

"That's no problem," Alan said. "But how are we going to get across that trench? I have the impression that ditch is still hot!"

"And I know it stinks," Ann said.

"We'll jump from the back end of the container that brought us here," Jongor said. "It overhangs the trench—"

He went first, clearing the hot trench easily. Alan followed, with Jongor giving the youth a hand. Ann came last. Jongor and Alan both reached helping hands toward her.

They went quickly across the caven. "I know how I got here," Alan said. "I marked the walls so I could find my way back up."

His marks were still on the walls. They went up quickly, rising level after level, until Jongor stopped to listen.

"What is it?" Ann asked.

"Murtos," he said. "We are being followed." He shook his head and indicated the crystal on his wrist. "If we can once get out of here and can find a dino sleeping in the swamps—"

"Hurry," Ann said. "The way I feel right now, riding a dino would be a pleasure."

They moved quickly forward. Ahead the tunnel widened into an open space. Light from above revealed Calazao there. Around him were Murto bodies. The giant was leaning on his axe.

At the sight of them, he lifted the axe. Jongor held up his hand, palm out.

"Peace, giant," he said. His eyes went to the bodies on the floor. "I see you know how to deal with those who do not pay their debts—"

"Yah!" Calazao grunted. "I will teach those Murtos to pay what is owed."

"We seek to pass in peace," Jongor said. "But behind us are Murtos who may still owe you something." With his thumb he gestured back along the tunnel through which he had come. "Hear them there?"

"Yah. I hear them!" the giant grumbled. Lowering his head, he peered into the tunnel.

While he was in a stooping position, Jongor, Alan, and Ann skipped past him.

"Good hunting, giant!" Jongor called back to him. Looking back, he saw that Murtos were already pouring from the tunnel and that the giant was now busy with his battle axe.

"Whew!" Alan Hunter said.

Moving quickly forward, they reached the exit from the ancient mines. A few Murtos were visible in the city but at the sight of those who had come back from the land of the Great Unknown God, the monkey-men fled hastily into hiding.

Jongor's eyes searched the swamp. Near the shore was something that looked like a floating island. At the sight of this, a grin came on his face. He concentrated his gaze on the crystal in the bracelet on his left wrist.

Moving, the island came ponderously to shore. There it snorted for directions.

"This way, little one," Jongor called to it.

The giant beast lifted its bulk over the broken wall of the Murto city. Coming to Jongor, it nuzzled against him. Gently he scratched it on the nose. The swamp monster almost purred with happiness.

Jongor turned anxiously to Ann Hunter. "Are you sure you can ride a dinosaur in comfort?" he asked. Concern was on his face and in his voice.

"Help me up, man from the jungle," Ann Hunter answered. "I never saw a limousine that looked as good to me as this swamp monster!"

The smile on her face wiped away all the concern from his voice. He lifted her up. Alan was already up.

"Move, monster!" Alan was shouting. "We've got places to go and things to see. Or I have. From the way my sister and Jongor are acting, I doubt if they can see anything except each other!"